TOM SAWYER ABROAD

AND OTHER STORIES

BY

MARK TWAIN

AUTHOR OF

THE ADVENTURES OF TOM SAWYER,
TOM SAWYER, DETECTIVE, ETC.

GROSSET & DUNLAP
PUBLISHERS   NEW YORK

Published by Arrangement with Harper & Brothers

CONTENTS

TOM SAWYER ABROAD

CHAPTER I

TOM SEEKS NEW ADVENTURES

DO you reckon Tom Sawyer was satisfied after all them adventures? I mean the adventures we had down the river, and the time we set the darky Jim free and Tom got shot in the leg. No, he wasn't. It only just p'isoned him for more. That was all the effect it had. You see, when we three came back up the river in glory, as you may say, from that long travel, and the village received us with a torchlight procession and speeches, and everybody hurrah'd and shouted, it made us heroes, and that was what Tom Sawyer had always been hankering to be.

For a while he *was* satisfied. Everybody made much of him, and he tilted up his nose and stepped around the town as though he owned it. Some called him Tom Sawyer the Traveler, and that just swelled him up fit to bust. You see he laid over me and Jim considerable, because we only went down the river on a raft and came back by the steamboat, but Tom went by the steamboat both ways. The boys envied me and Jim a good deal, but land! they just knuckled to the dirt before TOM.

Well, I don't know; maybe he might have been satisfied if it hadn't been for old Nat Parsons, which was postmaster, and powerful long and slim, and kind o' good-hearted and silly, and bald-headed, on account of his age, and about the talkiest old cretur I ever see. For as much as thirty years he'd been the only man in the village that had a reputation—I mean a reputation for being a traveler, and of course he was mortal proud of it, and it was reckoned that in the course of that thirty years he had told about that journey over a million times and enjoyed it every time. And now comes along a boy not quite fifteen, and sets everybody admiring and gawking over *his* travels, and it just give the poor old man the high strikes. It made him sick to listen to Tom, and to hear the people say "My land!" "Did you ever!" "My goodness sakes alive!" and all such things; but he couldn't pull away from it, any more than a fly that's got its hind leg fast in the molasses. And always when Tom come to a rest, the poor old cretur would chip in on *his* same old travels and work them for all they were worth; but they were pretty faded, and didn't go for much, and it was pitiful to see. And then Tom would take another innings, and then the old man again—and so on, and so on, for an hour and more, each trying to beat out the other.

You see, Parsons' travels happened like this: When he first got to be postmaster and was green in the business, there come a letter for somebody he didn't know, and there wasn't any such person in the village. Well, he didn't know what to do, nor how to act, and there the letter stayed and stayed, week in and week out, till the bare sight of it gave him a conniption. The postage wasn't paid on it, and that was another thing to worry about. There wasn't any way to collect that ten cents, and he reckoned the gov'ment would hold him responsible for it and maybe turn him out besides, when they found he hadn't collected it. Well, at last he couldn't stand it any longer. He couldn't sleep nights, he couldn't eat, he was thinned down to a shadder, yet he da'sn't ask anybody's advice, for the very person he asked for advice might go back on him and let the gov'-ment know about the letter. He had the letter buried under the floor, but that did no good; if he happened to see a person standing over the place it 'd give him the cold shivers, and loaded him up with suspicions, and he would sit up that night till the town was still and dark, and then he would sneak there and get it out and bury it in another place. Of course, people got to avoiding him and shaking their heads and whispering, because, the way he was look-ing and acting, they judged he had killed somebody or done something terrible, they didn't know what, and if he had been a stranger they would 've lynched him.

Well, as I was saying, it got so he couldn't stand it any longer; so he made up his mind to pull out for Washington, and just go to the President of the United States and make a clean breast of the whole thing, not keeping back an atom, and then fetch the letter out and lay it before the whole gov'ment, and say, "Now, there she is—do with me what you're a mind to; though as heaven is my judge I am an innocent man and not deserving of the full penalties of the law and leaving behind me a family that must starve and yet hadn't a thing to do with it, which is the whole truth and I can swear to it."

So he did it. He had a little wee bit of steamboating, and some stage-coaching, but all the rest of the way was horseback, and it took him three weeks to get to Washington. He saw lots of land and lots of villages and four cities. He was gone 'most eight weeks, and there never was such a proud man in the village as he when he got back. His travels made him the greatest man in all that region, and the most talked about; and people come from as much as thirty miles back in the country, and from over in the Illinois bottoms, too, just to look at him—and there they'd stand and gawk, and he'd gabble. You never see anything like it.

Well, there wasn't any way now to settle which was the greatest traveler; some said it was Nat, some said it was Tom. Everybody allowed that Nat had seen the most longitude, but they had to give in that whatever Tom was short in longitude he had made up in latitude and climate. It was about a stand-off; so both of them had to whoop up their dangerous adventures, and try to get ahead *that* way. That bullet-wound in Tom's leg was a tough thing for Nat Parsons to buck against, but he bucked the best he could; and at a disadvantage, too, for Tom didn't set still as he'd orter done, to be fair, but always got up and sauntered around and worked his limp while Nat was painting up the adventure that *he* had in Washington; for Tom never let go that limp when his leg got well, but practised it nights at home, and kept it good as new right along.

Nat's adventure was like this; I don't know how true it is: maybe he got it out of a paper, or somewhere, but I will say this for him, that he *did* know how to tell it. He could make anybody's flesh crawl, and he'd turn pale and hold his breath when he told it, and sometimes women and girls got so faint they couldn't stick it out. Well, it was this way, as near as I can remember:

He come a-loping into Washington, and put up his horse and shoved out to the President's house with his letter, and they told him the President was up to the Capitol, and just going to start for Philadelphia—not a minute to lose if he wanted to catch him. Nat 'most dropped, it made him so sick. His horse was put up, and he didn't know what *to* do. But just then along comes a darky driving an old ramshackly hack, and he see his chance. He rushes out and shouts: "A half a dollar if you git me to the Capitol in half an hour, and a quarter extra if you do it in twenty minutes!"

"Done!" says the darky.

Nat he jumped in and slammed the door, and away they went a-ripping and a-tearing over the roughest road a body ever see, and the racket of it was something awful. Nat passed his arms through the loops and hung on for life and death, but pretty soon the hack hit a rock and flew up in the air, and the bottom fell out, and when it come down Nat's feet was on the ground, and he see he was in the mos⸏ ⸏sperate danger if he couldn't keep up with the ⸏ ⸏. He was horrible scared, but he laid into his ⸏rk for all he was worth, and hung tight to the arm-loops and made his legs fairly fly. He yelled and shouted to the driver to stop, and so did the crowds along the street, for they could see his legs spinning along under the coach, and his head and shoulders bobbing inside through the windows, and he was in awful danger; but the more they all shouted the more the nigger whooped and yelled and lashed the horses and shouted, "Don't you fret, I'se gwine to git you dah in time, boss; I's gwine to do it, sho'!" for you see he thought they were all hurrying him up, and, of course, he couldn't hear anything for the racket he was making. And so they went ripping along, and everybody just petrified to see it; and when they got to the Capitol at last it was the quickest trip that ever was made, and everybody said so. The horses laid down, and Nat dropped, all tuckered out, and he was all dust and rags and barefooted; but he was in time and just in time, and caught the President and give him the letter, and everything was all right, and the President give him a free pardon on the spot, and Nat give the nigger two extra quarters instead of one, because he could see that if he hadn't had the hack he wouldn't 'a' got there in time, nor anywhere near it.

It *was* a powerful good adventure, and Tom Sawyer had to work his bullet-wound mighty lively to hold his own against it.

Well, by and by Tom's glory got to paling down

gradu'ly, on account of other things turning up for the people to talk about—first a horse-race, and on top of that a house afire, and on top of that the circus, and on top of that the eclipse; and that started a revival, same as it always does, and by that time there wasn't any more talk about Tom, so to speak, and you never see a person so sick and disgusted.

Pretty soon he got to worrying and fretting right along day in and day out, and when I asked him what *was* he in such a state about, he said it 'most broke his heart to think how time was slipping away, and him getting older and older, and no wars breaking out and no way of making a name for himself that he could see. Now that is the way boys is always thinking, but he was the first one I ever heard come out and say it.

So then he set to work to get up a plan to make him celebrated; and pretty soon he struck it, and offered to take me and Jim in. Tom Sawyer was always free and generous that way. There's a-plenty of boys that's mighty good and friendly when *you've* got a good thing, but when a good thing happens to come their way they don't say a word to you, and try to hog it all. That warn't ever Tom Sawyer's way, I can say that for him. There's plenty of boys that will come hankering and groveling around you when you've got an apple and beg the core off of you; but when they've got one, and you beg for the core and remind them how you give them a core one time, they say thank you 'most to death, but there ain't a-going to be no core. But I notice they always git come up with; all you got to do is to wait.

Well, we went out in the woods on the hill, and Tom told us what it was. It was a crusade.

"What's a crusade?" I says.

He looked scornful, the way he's always done when he was ashamed of a person, and says:

"Huck Finn, do you mean to tell me you don't know what a crusade is?"

"No," says I, "I don't. And I don't care to, nuther. I've lived till now and done without it, and had my health, too. But as soon as you tell me, I'll know, and that's soon enough. I don't see any use in finding out things and clogging up my head with them when I mayn't ever have any occasion to use 'em. There was Lance Williams, he learned how to talk Choctaw here till one come and dug his grave for him. Now, then, what's a crusade? But I can tell you one thing before you begin; if it's a patent-right, there's no money in it. Bill Thompson he—"

"Patent-right!" says he. "I never see such an idiot. Why, a crusade is a kind of war."

I thought he must be losing his mind. But no, he was in real earnest, and went right on, perfectly ca'm.

"A crusade is a war to recover the Holy Land from the paynim."

"Which Holy Land?"

"Why, *the* Holy Land—there ain't but one."

"What do *we* want of it?"

"Why, can't you understand? It's in the hands

of the paynim, and it's our duty to take it away from them."

"How did we come to let them git hold of it?"

"We didn't come to let them git hold of it. They always had it."

"Why, Tom, then it must belong to them, don't it?"

"Why, of course it does. Who said it didn't?"

I studied over it, but couldn't seem to git at the right of it, no way. I says:

"It's too many for me, Tom Sawyer. If I had a farm and it was mine, and another person wanted it, would it be right for him to—"

"Oh, shucks! you don't know enough to come in when it rains, Huck Finn. It ain't a farm, it's entirely different. You see, it's like this. They own the land, just the mere land, and that's all they *do* own; but it was our folks, our Jews and Christians, that made it holy, and so they haven't any business to be there defiling it. It's a shame, and we ought not to stand it a minute. We ought to march against them and take it away from them."

"Why, it does seem to me it's the most mixed-up thing I ever see! Now, if I had a farm and another person—"

"Don't I tell you it hasn't got anything to do with farming? Farming is business, just common low-down business: that's all it/is, it's all you can say for it; but this is higher, this is religious, and totally different."

"Religious to go and take the land away from people that owns it?"

9

"Certainly; it's always been considered so."

Jim he shook his head, and says:

"Mars Tom, I reckon dey's a mistake about it somers—dey mos' sholy is. I's religious myself, en I knows plenty religious people, but I hain't run across none dat acts like dat."

It made Tom hot, and he says:

"Well, it's enough to make a body sick, such mullet-headed ignorance! If either of you'd read anything about history, you'd know that Richard Cur de Loon, and the Pope, and Godfrey de Bulleyn, and lots more of the most noble-hearted and pious people in the world, hacked and hammered at the paynims for more than two hundred years trying to take their land away from them, and swum neck-deep in blood the whole time—and yet here's a couple of sap-headed country yahoos out in the backwoods of Missouri setting themselves up to know more about the rights and wrongs of it than they did! Talk about cheek!"

Well, of course, that put a more different light on it, and me and Jim felt pretty cheap and ignorant, and wished we hadn't been quite so chipper. I couldn't say nothing, and Jim he couldn't for a while; then he says:

"Well, den, I reckon it's all right; beca'se ef dey didn't know, dey ain't no use for po' ignorant folks like us to be trying to know; en so, ef it's our duty, we got to go en tackle it en do de bes' we can. Same time, I feel as sorry for dem paynims as Mars Tom. De hard part gwine to be to kill folks dat a body hain't been 'quainted wid and dat hain't done him

no harm. Dat's it, you see. Ef we wuz to go
'mongst 'em, jist we three, en say we's hungry, en
ast 'em for a bite to eat, why, maybe dey's jist like
yuther people. Don't you reckon dey is? Why,
dey'd give it, I know dey would, en den—"

"Then what?"

"Well, Mars Tom, my idea is like dis. It ain't no
use, we *can't* kill dem po' strangers dat ain't doin' us
no harm, till we've had practice—I knows it perfectly well, Mars Tom—'deed I knows it perfectly
well. But ef we takes a' ax or two, jist you en me
en Huck, en slips acrost de river to-night arter de
moon's gone down, en kills dat sick fam'ly dat's
over on the Sny, en burns dey house down, en—"

"Oh, you make me tired!" says Tom. "I don't
want to argue any more with people like you and
Huck Finn, that's always wandering from the subject, and ain't got any more sense than to try to
reason out a thing that's pure theology by the laws
that protect real estate!"

Now that's just where Tom Sawyer warn't fair.
Jim didn't mean no harm, and I didn't mean no
harm. We knowed well enough that he was right
and we was wrong, and all we was after was to get
at the *how* of it, and that was all; and the only reason he couldn't explain it so we could understand it
was because we was ignorant—yes, and pretty dull,
too, I ain't denying that; but, land! that ain't no
crime, I should think.

But he wouldn't hear no more about it—just said
if we had tackled the thing in the proper spirit, he
would 'a' raised a couple of thousand knights and

put them in steel armor from head to heel, and made me a lieutenant and Jim a sutler, and took the command himself and brushed the whole paynim outfit into the sea like flies and come back across the world in a glory like sunset. But he said we didn't know enough to take the chance when we had it, and he wouldn't ever offer it again. And he didn't. When he once got set, you couldn't budge him.

But I didn't care much. I am peaceable, and don't get up rows with people that ain't doing nothing to me. I allowed if the paynim was satisfied I was, and we would let it stand at that.

Now Tom he got all that notion out of Walter Scott's book, which he was always reading. And it *was* a wild notion, because in my opinion he never could 've raised the men, and if he did, as like as not he would 've got licked. I took the book and read all about it, and as near as I could make it out, most of the folks that shook farming to go crusading had a mighty rocky time of it.

CHAPTER II

WELL, Tom got up one thing after another, but they all had tender spots about 'em somewheres, and he had to shove 'em aside. So at last he was about in despair. Then the St. Louis papers begun to talk a good deal about the balloon that was going to sail to Europe, and Tom sort of thought he wanted to go down and see what it looked like, but couldn't make up his mind. But the papers went on talking, and so he allowed that maybe if he didn't go he mightn't ever have another chance to see a balloon; and next, he found out that Nat Parsons was going down to see it, and that decided him, of course. He wasn't going to have Nat Parsons coming back bragging about seeing the balloon, and him having to listen to it and keep quiet. So he wanted me and Jim to go too, and we went.

It was a noble big balloon, and had wings and fans and all sorts of things, and wasn't like any balloon you see in pictures. It was away out toward the edge of town, in a vacant lot, corner of Twelfth Street; and there was a big crowd around it, making fun of it, and making fun of the man—a lean pale feller with that soft kind of moonlight in his eyes, you know—and they kept saying it wouldn't go.

13

It made him hot to hear them, and he would turn on them and shake his fist and say they was animals and blind, but some day they would find they had stood face to face with one of the men that lifts up nations and makes civilizations, and was too dull to know it; and right here on this spot their own children and grandchildren would build a monument to him that would outlast a thousand years, but his name would outlast the monument. And then the crowd would burst out in a laugh again, and yell at him, and ask him what was his name before he was married, and what he would take to not do it, and what was his sister's cat's grandmother's name, and all the things that a crowd says when they've got hold of a feller that they see they can plague. Well, some things they said *was* funny—yes, and mighty witty too, I ain't denying that—but all the same it warn't fair nor brave, all them people pitching on one, and they so glib and sharp, and him without any gift of talk to answer back with. But, good land! what did he want to sass back for? You see, it couldn't do him no good, and it was just nuts for them. They *had* him, you know. But that was his way. I reckon he couldn't help it; he was made so, I judge. He was a good enough sort of cretur, and hadn't no harm in him, and was just a genius, as the papers said, which wasn't his fault. We can't all be sound: we've got to be the way we're made. As near as I can make out, geniuses think they know it all, and so they won't take people's advice, but always go their own way, which makes everybody forsake them and despise them, and that is perfectly natural. If they was humbler, and listened and tried to learn, it would be better for them.

The part the professor was in was like a boat, and was big and roomy, and had water-tight lockers around the inside to keep all sorts of things in, and a body could sit on them, and make beds on them, too. We went aboard, and there was twenty people there, snooping around and examining, and old Nat Parsons was there, too. The professor kept fussing around getting ready, and the people went ashore, drifting out one at a time, and old Nat he was the last. Of course it wouldn't do to let him go out behind *us*. We mustn't budge till he was gone, so we could be last ourselves.

But he was gone now, so it was time for us to follow. I heard a big shout, and turned around— the city was dropping from under us like a shot! It made me sick all through, I was so scared. Jim turned gray and couldn't say a word, and Tom didn't say nothing, but looked excited. The city went on dropping down, and down, and down; but we didn't seem to be doing nothing but just hang in the air and stand still. The houses got smaller and smaller, and the city pulled itself together, closer and closer, and the men and wagons got to looking like ants and bugs crawling around, and the streets like threads and cracks; and then it all kind of melted together, and there wasn't any city any more: it was only a big scar on the earth, and it seemed to me a body could see up the river and down the river about a thousand miles, though of course it wasn't so much. By and by the earth was a ball—just a round ball, of a dull color, with shiny stripes wriggling and winding around over it, which was rivers. The Widder Douglas always told me the earth was round like a ball, but I never took any stock in a lot of them superstitions o' hers, and of course I paid no attention to that one, because I could see myself that the world was the shape of a plate, and flat. I used to go up on the hill, and take a look around, and prove it for myself, because I reckon the best way to get a sure thing on a fact is to go and examine for yourself, and not take anybody's say-so. But I had to give in now that the widder was right. That is, she was right as to the rest of the world, but she warn't right about the part our village is in; that part is the shape of a plate, and flat, I take my oath!

The professor had been quiet all this time, as if he was asleep; but he broke loose now, and he was mighty bitter. He says something like this:

"Idiots! They said it wouldn't go; and they wanted to examine it, and spy around and get the secret of it out of me. But I beat them. Nobody knows the secret but me. Nobody knows what makes it move but me; and it's a new power—a new power, and a thousand times the strongest in the earth! Steam's foolishness to it! They said I couldn't go to Europe. To Europe! Why, there's power aboard to last five years, and feed for three months. They are fools! What do they know about it? Yes, and they said my airship was flimsy. Why, she's good for fifty years! I can sail the skies all my life if I want to, and steer where I please, though they laughed at that, and said I couldn't.

Couldn't steer! Come here, boy; we'll see. **You** press these buttons as I tell you."

He made Tom steer the ship all about and every which way, and learnt him the whole thing in nearly no time; and Tom said it was perfectly easy. He made him fetch the ship down 'most to the earth, and had him spin her along so close to the Illinois prairies that a body could talk to the farmers, and hear everything they said perfectly plain; and he flung out printed bills to them that told about the balloon, and said it was going to Europe. Tom got so he could steer straight for a tree till he got nearly to it, and then dart up and skin right along over the top of it. Yes, and he showed Tom how to land her; and he done it first-rate, too, and set her down in the prairies as soft as wool. But the minute we started to skip out the professor says, "No, you don't!" and shot her up in the air again. It was awful. I begun to beg, and so did Jim; but it only give his temper a rise, and he begun to rage around and look wild out of his eyes, and I was scared of him.

Well, then he got on to his troubles again, and mourned and grumbled about the way he was treated, and couldn't seem to git over it, and especially people's saying his ship was flimsy. He scoffed at that, and at their saying she warn't simple and would be always getting out of order. Get out of order! That graveled him; he said that she couldn't any more get out of order than the solar sister.

He got worse and worse, and I never see a person take on so. It give me the cold shivers to see him, and so it did Jim. By and by he got to yelling and screaming, and then he swore the world shouldn't ever have his secret at all now, it had treated him so mean. He said he would sail his balloon around the globe just to show what he could do, and then he would sink it in the sea, and sink us all along with it, too. Well, it was the awfulest fix to be in, and here was night coming on!

He give us something to eat, and made us go to the other end of the boat, and he laid down on a locker, where he could boss all the works, and put his old pepper-box revolver under his head, and said if anybody come fooling around there trying to land her, he would kill him.

We set scrunched up together, and thought considerable, but didn't say much—only just a word once in a while when a body had to say something or bust, we was *so* scared and worried. The night dragged along slow and lonesome. We was pretty low down, and the moonshine made everything soft and pretty, and the farmhouses looked snug and homeful, and we could hear the farm sounds, and wished we could be down there; but, laws! we just slipped along over them like a ghost, and never left a track.

Away in the night, when all the sounds was late sounds, and the air had a late feel, and a late smell, too—about a two-o'clock feel, as near as I could make out—Tom said the professor was so quiet this time he must be asleep, and we'd better—

"Better what?" I says in a whisper, and feeling sick all over, because I knowed what he was thinking about.

"Better slip back there and tie him, and land the ship," he says.

I says: "No, sir! Don't you budge, Tom Sawyer."

And Jim—well, Jim was kind o' gasping, he was so scared. He says:

"Oh, Mars Tom, *don't!* Ef you teches him, we's gone—we's gone sho'! I ain't gwine anear him, not for nothin' in dis worl'. Mars Tom, he's plumb crazy."

Tom whispers and says: "That's *why* we've got to do something. If he wasn't crazy I wouldn't give shucks to be anywhere but here; you couldn't hire me to get out—now that I've got used to this balloon and over the scare of being cut loose from the solid ground—if he was in his right mind. But it's no good politics, sailing around like this with a person that's out of his head, and says he's going round the world and then drown us all. We've *got* to do something, I tell you, and do it before he wakes up, too, or we mayn't ever get another chance. Come!"

But it made us turn cold and creepy just to think of it, and we said we wouldn't budge. So Tom was for slipping back there by himself to see if he couldn't get at the steering-gear and land the ship. We begged and begged him not to, but it warn't no use; so he got down on his hands and knees, and begun to crawl an inch at a time, we a-holding our breath and watching. After he got to the middle of the boat he crept slower than ever, and it did seem like years to me. But at last we see him get to the professor's head, and sort of raise up soft and look a good spell in his face and listen. Then we see him begin to inch along again toward the professor's feet where the steering-buttons was. Well, he got there all safe, and was reaching slow and steady toward the buttons, but he knocked down something that made a noise, and we see him slump down flat an' soft in the bottom, and lay still. The professor stirred, and says, "What's that?" But everybody kept dead still and quiet, and he begun to mutter and mumble and nestle, like a person that's going to wake up, and I thought I was going to die, I was so worried and scared.

Then a cloud slid over the moon, and I 'most cried, I was so glad. She buried herself deeper and deeper into the cloud, and it got so dark we couldn't see Tom. Then it began to sprinkle rain, and we could hear the professor fussing at his ropes and things and abusing the weather. We was afraid every minute he would touch Tom, and then we would be goners, and no help; but Tom was already on his way back, and when we felt his hands on our knees my breath stopped sudden, and my heart fell down 'mongst my other works, because I couldn't tell in the dark but it might be the professor, which I thought it *was*.

Dear! I was so glad to have him back that I was just as near happy as a person could be that was up in the air that way with a deranged man. You can't land a balloon in the dark, and so I hoped it would keep on raining, for I didn't want Tom to go meddling any more and make us so awful uncomfortable. Well, I got my wish. It drizzled and drizzled along the rest of the night, which wasn't long, though it did seem so; and at daybreak it cleared, and the world looked mighty soft and gray and pretty, and the forests and fields so good to see again, and the horses and cattle standing sober and thinking. Next, the sun come a-blazing up gay and splendid, and then we began to feel rusty and stretchy, and first we knowed we was all asleep.

CHAPTER III

TOM EXPLAINS

WE went to sleep about four o'clock, and woke up about eight. The professor was setting back there at his end, looking glum. He pitched us some breakfast, but he told us not to come abaft the midship compass. That was about the middle of the boat. Well, when you are sharp-set, and you eat and satisfy yourself, everything looks pretty different from what it done before. It makes a body feel pretty near comfortable, even when he is up in a balloon with a genius. We got to talking together.

There was one thing that kept bothering me, and by and by I says:

"Tom, didn't we start east?"

"Yes."

"How fast have we been going?"

"Well, you heard what the professor said when he was raging round. Sometimes, he said, we was making fifty miles an hour, sometimes ninety, sometimes a hundred; said that with a gale to help he could make three hundred any time, and said if he wanted the gale, and wanted it blowing the right direction, he only had to go up higher or down lower to find it."

"Well, then, it's just as I reckoned. The professor lied."

"Why?"

"Because if we was going so fast we ought to be past Illinois, oughtn't we?"

"Certainly."

"Well, we ain't."

"What's the reason we ain't?"

"I know by the color. We're right over Illinois yet. And you can see for yourself that Indiana ain't in sight."

"I wonder what's the matter with you, Huck. You know by the *color*?"

"Yes, of course I do."

"What's the color got to do with it?"

"It's got everything to do with it. Illinois is green, Indiana is pink. You show me any pink down here, if you can. No, sir; it's green."

"Indiana *pink*? Why, what a lie!"

"It ain't no lie; I've seen it on the map, and it's pink."

You never see a person so aggravated and disgusted. He says:

"Well, if I was such a numskull as you, Huck Finn, I would jump over. Seen it on the map! Huck Finn, did you reckon the states was the same color out-of-doors as they are on the map?"

"Tom Sawyer, what's a map for? Ain't it to learn you facts?"

"Of course."

"Well, then, how's it going to do that if it tells lies? That's what I want to know."

"Shucks, you muggins! It don't tell lies."

"It don't, don't it?"

"No, it don't."

"All right, then; if it don't, there ain't no two states the same color. You git around *that*, if you can, Tom Sawyer."

He see I had him, and Jim see it too; and I tell you, I felt pretty good, for Tom Sawyer was always a hard person to git ahead of. Jim slapped his leg and says:

"I tell *you!* dat's smart, dat's right down smart. Ain't no use, Mars Tom; he got you *dis* time, sho'!" He slapped his leg again, and says, "My *lan'*, but it was smart one!"

I never felt so good in my life; and yet *I* didn't know I was saying anything much till it was out. I was just mooning along, perfectly careless, and not expecting anything was going to happen, and never *thinking* of such a thing at all, when, all of a sudden, out it came. Why, it was just as much a surprise to me as it was to any of them. It was just the same way it is when a person is munching along on a hunk of corn-pone, and not thinking about anything, and all of a sudden bites into a di'mond. Now all that *he* knows first off is that it's some kind of gravel he's bit into; but he don't find out it's a di'mond till he gits it out and brushes off the sand and crumbs and one thing or another, and has a look at it, and then he's surprised and glad—yes, and proud too; though when you come to look the thing straight in the eye, he ain't entitled to as much credit as he would 'a' been if he'd been *hunting* di'monds. You can see the difference easy if you think it over. You see, an accident, that way, ain't fairly as big a thing as a thing that's done a-purpose. Anybody could find that di'mond in that corn-pone; but mind you, it's got to be somebody that's got *that kind of a corn-pone*. That's where that feller's credit comes in, you see; and that's where mine comes in. I don't claim no great things—I don't reckon I could 'a' done it again—but I done it that time; that's all I claim. And I hadn't no more idea I could do such a thing, and warn't any more thinking about it or trying to, than you be this minute. Why, I was just as ca'm, a body couldn't be any ca'mer, and yet, all of a sudden, out it come. I've often thought of that time, and I can remember just the way everything looked, same as if it was only last week. I can see it all: beautiful rolling country with woods and fields and lakes for hundreds and hundreds of miles all around, and towns and villages scattered everywheres under us, here and there and yonder; and the professor mooning over a chart on his little table, and Tom's cap flopping in the rigging where it was hung up to dry. And one thing in particular was a bird right alongside, not ten foot off, going our way and trying to keep up, but losing ground all the time; and a railroad-train doing the same thing down there, sliding among the trees and farms, and pouring out a long cloud of black smoke and now and then a little puff of white; and when the white was gone so long you had almost forgot it, you would hear a little faint toot, and that was the whistle. And we left the bird and the train both behind, *'way* behind, and done it easy, too.

But Tom he was huffy, and said me and Jim was

a couple of ignorant blatherskites, and then he says:

"Suppose there's a brown calf and a big brown dog, and an artist is making a picture of them. What is the *main* thing that that artist has got to do? He has got to paint them so you can tell them apart the minute you look at them, hain't he? Of course. Well, then, do you want him to go and paint *both* of them brown? Certainly you don't. He paints one of them blue, and then you can't make no mistake. It's just the same with the maps. That's why they make every state a different color; it ain't to deceive you, it's to keep you from deceiving yourself."

But I couldn't see no argument about that, and neither could Jim. Jim shook his head, and says:

"Why, Mars Tom, if you knowed what chuckle-heads dem painters is, you'd wait a long time before you'd fetch one er *dem* in to back up a fac'. I's gwine to tell you, den you kin see for you'self. I see one of 'em a-paintin' away, one day, down in ole Hank Wilson's back lot, en I went down to see, en he was paintin' dat old brindle cow wid de near horn gone—you knows de one I means. En I ast him what he's paintin' her for, en he say when he git her painted, de picture's wuth a hundred dollars. Mars Tom, he could 'a' got de cow fer fifteen, en I *tole* him so. Well, sah, if you'll b'lieve me, he jes' shuck his head, dat painter did, en went on a-dobbin'. Bless you, Mars Tom, *dey* don't know nothin'."

Tom lost his temper. I notice a person 'most always does that's got laid out in an argument. He told us to shut up, and maybe we'd feel better.

Then he see a town clock away off down yonder, and he took up the glass and looked at it, and then looked at his silver turnip, and then at the clock, and then at the turnip again, and says:

"That's funny! That clock's near about an hour fast."

So he put up his turnip. Then he see another clock, and took a look, and it was an hour fast too. That puzzled him.

"That's a mighty curious thing," he says. "I don't understand it."

Then he took the glass and hunted up another clock, and sure enough it was an hour fast too. Then his eyes began to spread and his breath to come out kinder gaspy like, and he says:

"Ger-reat Scott, it's the *longitude!*"

I says, considerably scared:

"Well, what's been and gone and happened now?"

"Why, the thing that's happened is that this old bladder has slid over Illinois and Indiana and Ohio like nothing, and this is the east end of Pennsylvania or New York, or somewheres around there."

"Tom Sawyer, you don't mean it!"

"Yes, I do, and it's dead sure. We've covered about fifteen degrees of longitude since we left St. Louis yesterday afternoon, and them clocks are *right*. We've come close on to eight hundred miles."

I didn't believe it, but it made the cold streaks trickle down my back just the same. In my experience I knowed it wouldn't take much short of two weeks to do it down the Mississippi on a raft.

Jim was working his mind and studying. Pretty soon he says:

"Mars Tom, did you say dem clocks uz right?"

"Yes, they're right."

"Ain't yo' watch right, too?"

"She's right for St. Louis, but she's an hour wrong for here."

"Mars Tom, is you tryin' to let on dat de time ain't de *same* everywheres?"

"No, it ain't the same everywheres, by a long shot."

Jim looked distressed, and says:

"It grieves me to hear you talk like dat, Mars Tom; I's right down ashamed to hear you talk like dat, arter de way you's been raised. Yassir, it 'd break yo' Aunt Polly's heart to hear you."

Tom was astonished. He looked Jim over wondering, and didn't say nothing, and Jim went on:

"Mars Tom, who put de people out yonder in St. Louis? De Lord done it. Who put de people here whar we is? De Lord done it. Ain' dey bofe his children? 'Cose dey is. *Well*, den! is he gwine to *scriminate* 'twixt 'em?"

"Scriminate! I never heard such ignorance. There ain't no discriminating about it. When he makes you and some more of his children black, and makes the rest of us white, what do you call that?"

Jim see the p'int. He was stuck. He couldn't answer. Tom says:

"He does discriminate, you see, when he wants to; but this case *here* ain't no discrimination of his, it's man's. The Lord made the day, and he made the night; but he didn't invent the hours, and he didn't distribute them around. Man did that."

"Mars Tom, is dat so? Man done it?"

"Certainly."

"Who tole him he could?"

"Nobody. He never asked."

Jim studied a minute, and says:

"Well, dat do beat me. I wouldn't 'a' tuck no sich resk. But some people ain't scared o' nothin'. Dey bangs right ahead; *dey* don't care what happens. So den dey's allays an hour's diff'unce everywhah, Mars Tom?"

"An hour? No! It's four minutes difference for every degree of longitude, you know. Fifteen of 'em's an hour, thirty of 'em's two hours, and so on. When it's one o'clock Tuesday morning in England, it's eight o'clock the night before in New York."

Jim moved a little way along the locker, and you could see he was insulted. He kept shaking his head and muttering, and so I slid along to him and patted him on the leg, and petted him up, and got him over the worst of his feelings, and then he says:

"Mars Tom talkin' sich talk as dat! Choosday in one place en Monday in t'other, bofe in the same day! Huck, dis ain't no place to joke—up here whah we is. Two days in one day! How you gwine to get two days inter one day? Can't git two hours inter one hour, kin you? Can't git two niggers inter one nigger skin, kin you? Can't git two gallons of whisky inter a one-gallon jug, kin you? No, sir, 'twould strain de jug. Yes, en even den you couldn't, *I* don't believe. Why, looky here, Huck, s'posen de Choosday was New Year's—now den! is you gwine to tell me it's dis year in one place en las' year in t'other, bofe in de identical same minute? It's de beatenest rubbage! I can't stan' it—I can't stan' to hear tell 'bout it." Then he begun to shiver and turn gray, and Tom says:

"*Now* what's the matter? What's the trouble?"

Jim could hardly speak, but he says:

"Mars Tom, you ain't jokin', en it's *so?*"

"No, I'm not, and it *is* so."

Jim shivered again, and says:

"Den dat Monday could be de las' day, en dey wouldn't be no las' day in England, en de dead wouldn't be called. We mustn't go over dah, Mars Tom. Please git him to turn back; I wants to be whah—"

All of a sudden we see something, and all jumped up, and forgot everything and begun to gaze. Tom says:

"Ain't that the—" He catched his breath, then says: "It *is*, sure as you live! It's the ocean!"

That made me and Jim catch our breath, too. Then we all stood petrified but happy, for none of us had ever seen an ocean, or ever expected to. Tom kept muttering:

"Atlantic Ocean—Atlantic. Land, don't it sound great! And that's *it*—and *we* are looking at it—we! Why, it's just too splendid to believe!"

Then we see a big bank of black smoke; and when we got nearer, it was a city—and a monster she was, too, with a thick fringe of ships around one edge; and we wondered if it was New York, and begun to jaw and dispute about it, and, first we knowed, it slid from under us and went flying behind, and here we was, out over the very ocean itself, and going like a cyclone. Then we woke up, I tell you!

We made a break aft and raised a wail, and begun to beg the professor to turn back and land us, but he jerked out his pistol and motioned us back, and we went, but nobody will ever know how bad we felt.

The land was gone, all but a little streak, like a snake, away off on the edge of the water, and down under us was just ocean, ocean, ocean—millions of miles of it, heaving and pitching and squirming, and white sprays blowing from the wave-tops, and only a few ships in sight, wallowing around and laying over, first on one side and then on t'other, and sticking their bows under and then their sterns; and before long there warn't no ships at all, and we had the sky and the whole ocean all to ourselves, and the roomiest place I ever see and the lonesomest.

CHAPTER IV

STORM

AND it got lonesomer and lonesomer. There was the big sky up there, empty and awful deep; and the ocean down there without a thing on it but just the waves. All around us was a ring, where the sky and the water come together; yes, a monstrous big ring it was, and we right in the dead center of it—plumb in the center. We was racing along like a prairie-fire, but it never made any difference, we couldn't seem to git past that center no way. I couldn't see that we ever gained an inch on that ring. It made a body feel creepy, it was so curious and unaccountable.

Well, everything was so awful still that we got to talking in a very low voice, and kept on getting creepier and lonesomer and less and less talky, till at last the talk ran dry altogether, and we just set there and "thunk," as Jim calls it, and never said a word the longest time.

The professor never stirred till the sun was overhead; then he stood up and put a kind of triangle to his eye, and Tom said it was a sextant and he was taking the sun to see whereabouts the balloon was. Then he ciphered a little and looked in a book, and then he begun to carry on again. He said lots of

32

wild things, and, among others, he said he would keep up this hundred-mile gait till the middle of to-morrow afternoon, and then he'd land in London.

We said we would be humbly thankful.

He was turning away, but he whirled around when we said that, and give us a long look of his blackest kind—one of the maliciousest and suspiciousest looks I ever see. Then he says:

"You want to leave me. Don't try to deny it."

We didn't know what to say, so we held in and didn't say nothing at all.

He went aft and set down, but he couldn't seem to git that thing out of his mind. Every now and then he would rip out something about it, and try to make us answer him, but we dasn't.

It got lonesomer and lonesomer right along, and it did seem to me I couldn't stand it. It was still worse when night begun to come on. By and by Tom pinched me and whispers:

"Look!"

I took a glance aft, and see the professor taking a whet out of a bottle. I didn't like the looks of that. By and by he took another drink, and pretty soon he begun to sing. It was dark now, and getting black and stormy. He went on singing, wilder and wilder, and the thunder begun to mutter, and the wind to wheeze and moan among the ropes, and altogether it was awful. It got so black we couldn't see him any more, and wished we couldn't hear him, but we could. Then he got still; but he warn't still ten minutes till we got suspicious, and wished he would start up his noise again, so we could tell where he was. By and by there was a flash of lightning, and we see him start to get up, but he staggered and fell down. We heard him scream out in the dark:

"They don't want to go to England. All right, I'll change the course. They want to leave me. I know they do. Well, they shall—and *now!*"

I 'most died when he said that. Then he was still again—still so long I couldn't bear it, and it did seem to me the lightning wouldn't *ever* come again. But at last there was a blessed flash, and there he was, on his hands and knees crawling, and not four feet from us. My, but his eyes was terrible! He made a lunge for Tom, and says, "Overboard *you* go!" but it was already pitch-dark again, and I couldn't see whether he got him or not, and Tom didn't make a sound.

There was another long, horrible wait; then there was a flash, and I see Tom's head sink down outside the boat and disappear. He was on the rope-ladder that dangled down in the air from the gunnel. The professor let off a shout and jumped for him, and straight off it was pitch-dark again, and Jim groaned out, "Po' Mars Tom, he's a goner!" and made a jump for the professor, but the professor warn't there.

Then we heard a couple of terrible screams, and then another not so loud, and then another that was 'way below, and you could only *just* hear it; and I heard Jim say, "Po' Mars Tom!"

Then it was awful still, and I reckon a person could 'a' counted four thousand before the next flash come. When it come I see Jim on his knees, with his arms on the locker and his face buried in them, and he was crying. Before I could look over the edge it was all dark again, and I was glad, because I didn't want to see. But when the next flash come, I was watching, and down there I see somebody a-swinging in the wind on the ladder, and it was Tom!

"Come up!" I shouts; "come up, Tom!"

His voice was so weak, and the wind roared so, I couldn't make out what he said, but I thought he asked was the professor up there. I shouts:

"No, he's down in the ocean! Come up! Can we help you?"

Of course, all this in the dark.

"Huck, who is you hollerin' at?"

"I'm hollerin' at Tom."

"Oh, Huck, how kin you act so, when you know po' Mars Tom—" Then he let off an awful scream, and flung his head and his arms back and let off another one, because there was a white glare just then, and he had raised up his face just in time to see Tom's, as white as snow, rise above the gunnel and look him right in the eye. He thought it was Tom's ghost, you see.

Tom clumb aboard, and when Jim found it *was* him, and not his ghost, he hugged him, and called him all sorts of loving names, and carried on like he was gone crazy, he was so glad. Says I:

"What did you wait for, Tom? Why didn't you come up at first?"

"I dasn't, Huck. I knowed somebody plunged down past me, but I didn't know who it was in the dark. It could 'a' been you, it could 'a' been Jim."

That was the way with Tom Sawyer—always

sound. He warn't coming up till he knowed where the professor was.

The storm let go about this time with all its might; and it was dreadful the way the thunder boomed and tore, and the lightning glared out, and the wind sung and screamed in the rigging, and the rain come down. One second you couldn't see your hand before you, and the next you could count the threads in your coat-sleeve, and see a whole wide desert of waves pitching and tossing through a kind of veil of rain. A storm like that is the loveliest thing there is, but it ain't at its best when you are up in the sky and lost, and it's wet and lonesome, and there's just been a death in the family.

We set there huddled up in the bow, and talked low about the poor professor; and everybody was sorry for him, and sorry the world had made fun of him and treated him so harsh, when he was doing the best he could, and hadn't a friend nor nobody to encourage him and keep him from brooding his mind away and going deranged. There was plenty of clothes and blankets and everything at the other end, but we thought we'd ruther take the rain than go meddling back there.

CHAPTER V

LAND

WE tried to make some plans, but we couldn't come to no agreement. Me and Jim was for turning around and going back home, but Tom allowed that by the time daylight come, so we could see our way, we would be so far toward England that we might as well go there, and come back in a ship, and have the glory of saying we done it.

About midnight the storm quit and the moon come out and lit up the ocean, and we begun to feel comfortable and drowsy; so we stretched out on the lockers and went to sleep, and never woke up again till sun-up. The sea was sparkling like di'monds, and it was nice weather, and pretty soon our things was all dry again.

We went aft to find some breakfast, and the first thing we noticed was that there was a dim light burning in a compass back there under a hood. Then Tom was disturbed. He says:

"You know what that means, easy enough. It means that somebody has got to stay on watch and steer this thing the same as he would a ship, or she'll wander around and go wherever the wind wants her to."

"Well," I says, "what's she been doing since— er—since we had the accident?"

"Wandering," he says, kinder troubled—"wandering, without any doubt. She's in a wind now that's blowing her south of east. We don't know how long that's been going on, either."

So then he p'inted her east, and said he would hold her there till we rousted out the breakfast. The professor had laid in everything a body could want; he couldn't 'a' been better fixed. There wasn't no milk for the coffee, but there was water, and everything else you could want, and a charcoal stove and the fixings for it, and pipes and cigars and matches; and wine and liquor, which warn't in our line; and books, and maps, and charts, and an accordion; and furs, and blankets, and no end of rubbish, like brass beads and brass jewelry, which Tom said was a sure sign that he had an idea of visiting among savages. There was money, too. Yes, the professor was well enough fixed.

After breakfast Tom learned me and Jim how to steer, and divided us all up into four-hour watches, turn and turn about; and when his watch was out I took his place, and he got out the professor's papers and pens and wrote a letter home to his aunt Polly, telling her everything that had happened to us, and dated it "*In the Welkin, approaching England*," and folded it together and stuck it fast with a red wafer, and directed it, and wrote above the direction, in big writing, "*From Tom Sawyer, the Erronort*," and said it would stump old Nat Parsons, the postmaster, when it come along in the mail. I says:

"Tom Sawyer, this ain't no welkin; it's a balloon."

"Well, now, who *said* it was a welkin, smarty?"

"You've wrote it on the letter, anyway."

"What of it? That don't mean that the balloon's the welkin."

"Oh, I thought it did. Well, then, what is a welkin?"

I see in a minute he was stuck. He raked and scraped around in his mind, but he couldn't find nothing, so he had to say:

"*I* don't know, and nobody don't know. It's just a word, and it's a mighty good word, too. There ain't many that lays over it. I don't believe there's *any* that does."

"Shucks!" I says. "But what does it *mean?*— that's the p'int."

"*I* don't know what it means, I tell you. It's a word that people uses for—for—well, it's ornamental. They don't put ruffles on a shirt to keep a person warm, do they?"

"Course they don't."

"But they put them *on*, don't they?"

"Yes."

"All right, then; that letter I wrote is a shirt, and the welkin's the ruffle on it."

I judged that that would gravel Jim, and it did.

"Now, Mars Tom, it ain't no use to talk like dat; en, moreover, it's sinful. You knows a letter ain't no shirt, en dey ain't no ruffles on it, nuther. Dey ain't no place to put 'em on; you can't put 'em on, and dey wouldn't stay ef you did."

"Oh, *do* shut up, and wait till something's started that you know something about."

"Why, Mars Tom, sholy you can't mean to say I

39

don't know about shirts, when, goodness knows, I's toted home de washin' ever sence—"

"I tell you, this hasn't got anything to *do* with shirts. I only—"

"Why, Mars Tom, you said yo'self dat a letter—"

"Do you want to drive me crazy? Keep still. I only used it as a metaphor."

That word kinder bricked us up for a minute. Then Jim says—rather timid, because he see Tom was getting pretty tetchy:

"Mars Tom, what is a metaphor?"

"A metaphor's a—well, it's a—a—a metaphor's an illustration." He see *that* didn't git home, so he tried again. "When I say birds of a feather flocks together, it's a metaphorical way of saying—"

"But dey *don't*, Mars Tom. No, sir, 'deed dey don't. Dey ain't no feathers dat's more alike den a bluebird en a jaybird, but ef you waits till you catches *dem* birds together, you'll—"

"Oh, give us a rest! You can't get the simplest little thing through your thick skull. Now don't bother me any more."

Jim was satisfied to stop. He was dreadful pleased with himself for catching Tom out. The minute Tom begun to talk about birds I judged he was a goner, because Jim knowed more about birds than both of us put together. You see, he had killed hundreds and hundreds of them, and that's the way to find out about birds. That's the way people does that writes books about birds, and loves them so that they'll go hungry and tired and take any amount of trouble to find a new bird and kill it. Their name is ornithologers, and I could have been an ornithologer myself, because I always loved birds and creatures; and I started out to learn how to be one, and I see a bird setting on a limb of a high tree, singing with its head tilted back and its mouth open, and before I thought I fired, and his song stopped and he fell straight down from the limb, all limp like a rag, and I run and picked him up and he was dead, and his body was warm in my hand, and his head rolled about this way and that, like his neck was broke, and there was a little white skin over his eyes, and one little drop of blood on the side of his head; and, laws! I couldn't see nothing more for the tears; and I hain't never murdered no creature since that warn't doing me no harm, and I ain't going to.

But I was aggravated about that welkin. I wanted to know. I got the subject up again, and then Tom explained, the best he could. He said when a person made a big speech the newspapers said the shouts of the people made the welkin ring. He said they always said that, but none of them ever told what it was, so he allowed it just meant outdoors and up high. Well, that seemed sensible enough, so I was satisfied, and said so. That pleased Tom and put him in a good humor again, and he says:

"Well, it's all right, then; and we'll let bygones be bygones. I don't know for certain what a welkin is, but when we land in London we'll make it ring, anyway, and don't you forget it."

He said an erronort was a person who sailed around in balloons; and said it was a mighty sight finer to be Tom Sawyer the Erronort than to be Tom

Sawyer the Traveler, and we would be heard of all round the world, if we pulled through all right, and so he wouldn't give shucks to be a traveler now.

Toward the middle of the afternoon we got everything ready to land, and we felt pretty good, too, and proud; and we kept watching with the glasses, like Columbus discovering America. But we couldn't see nothing but ocean. The afternoon wasted out and the sun shut down, and still there warn't no land anywheres. We wondered what was the matter, but reckoned it would come out all right, so we went on steering east, but went up on a higher level so we wouldn't hit any steeples or mountains in the dark.

It was my watch till midnight, and then it was Jim's; but Tom stayed up, because he said ship-captains done that when they was making the land, and didn't stand no regular watch.

Well, when daylight come, Jim give a shout, and we jumped up and looked over, and there was the land sure enough—land all around, as far as you could see, and perfectly level and yaller. We didn't know how long we'd been over it. There warn't no trees, nor hills, nor rocks, nor towns, and Tom and Jim had took it for the sea. They took it for the sea in a dead ca'm; but we was so high up, anyway, that if it had been the sea and rough, it would 'a' looked smooth, all the same, in the night, that way.

We was all in a powerful excitement now, and grabbed the glasses and hunted everywheres for London, but couldn't find hair nor hide of it, nor any other settlement—nor any sign of a lake or a river, either. Tom was clean beat. He said it warn't his notion of England; he thought England looked like America, and always had that idea. So he said we better have breakfast, and then drop down and inquire the quickest way to London. We cut the breakfast pretty short, we was so impatient. As we slanted along down, the weather began to moderate, and pretty soon we shed our furs. But it kept *on* moderating, and in a precious little while it was 'most too moderate. We was close down now, and just blistering!

We settled down to within thirty foot of the land—that is, it was land if sand is land; for this wasn't anything but pure sand. Tom and me clumb down the ladder and took a run to stretch our legs, and it felt amazing good—that is, the stretching did, but the sand scorched our feet like hot embers. Next, we see somebody coming, and started to meet him; but we heard Jim shout, and looked around and he was fairly dancing, and making signs, and yelling. We couldn't make out what he said, but we was scared anyway, and begun to heel it back to the balloon. When we got close enough, we understood the words, and they made me sick:

"Run! Run fo' yo' life! Hit's a lion; I kin see him thoo de glass! Run, boys; do please heel it de bes' you kin. He's bu'sted outen de menagerie, en dey ain't nobody to stop him!"

It made Tom fly, but it took the stiffening all out of my legs. I could only just gasp along the way you do in a dream when there's a ghost gaining on you.

Tom got to the ladder and shinned up it a piece

and waited for me; and as soon as I got a foothold on it he shouted to Jim to soar away. But Jim had clean lost his head, and said he had forgot how. So Tom shinned along up and told me to follow; but the lion was arriving, fetching a most ghastly roar with every lope, and my legs shook so I dasn't try to take one of them out of the rounds for fear the other one would give way under me.

But Tom was aboard by this time, and he started the balloon up a little, and stopped it again as soon as the end of the ladder was ten or twelve feet above ground. And there was the lion, a-ripping around under me, and roaring and springing up in the air at the ladder, and only missing it about a quarter of an inch, it seemed to me. It was delicious to be out of his reach, perfectly delicious, and made me feel good and thankful all up one side; but I was hanging there helpless and couldn't climb, and that made me feel perfectly wretched and miserable all down the other. It is most seldom that a person feels so mixed like that; and it is not to be recommended, either.

Tom asked me what he'd better do, but I didn't know. He asked me if I could hold on whilst he sailed away to a safe place and left the lion behind. I said I could if he didn't go no higher than he was now; but if he went higher I would lose my head and fall, sure. So he said, "Take a good grip," and he started.

"Don't go so fast," I shouted. "It makes my head swim."

He had started like a lightning express. He slowed

down, and we glided over the sand slower, but still in a kind of sickening way; for it *is* uncomfortable to see things sliding and gliding under you like that, and not a sound.

But pretty soon there was plenty of sound, for the lion was catching up. The noise fetched others. You could see them coming on the lope from every direction, and pretty soon there was a couple of dozen of them under me, jumping up at the ladder and snarling and snapping at each other; and so we went skinning along over the sand, and these fellers doing what they could to help us to not forgit the occasion; and then some other beasts come, without an invite, and they started a regular riot down there.

We see this plan was a mistake. We couldn't ever git away from them at this gait, and I couldn't hold on forever. So Tom took a think, and struck another idea. That was, to kill a lion with the pepper-box revolver, and then sail away while the others stopped to fight over the carcass. So he stopped the balloon still, and done it, and then we sailed off while the fuss was going on, and come down a quarter of a mile off, and they helped me aboard; but by the time we was out of reach again, that gang was on hand once more. And when they see we was really gone and they couldn't get us, they sat down on their hams and looked up at us so kind of disappointed that it was as much as a person could do not to see *their* side of the matter.

CHAPTER VI

IT'S A CARAVAN

I WAS so weak that the only thing I wanted was a chance to lay down, so I made straight for my locker-bunk, and stretched myself out there. But a body couldn't get back his strength in no such oven as that, so Tom give the command to soar, and Jim started her aloft.

We had to go up a mile before we struck comfortable weather where it was breezy and pleasant and just right, and pretty soon I was all straight again. Tom had been setting quiet and thinking; but now he jumps up and says:

"I bet you a thousand to one *I* know where we are. We're in the Great Sahara, as sure as guns!"

He was so excited he couldn't hold still; but I wasn't. I says:

"Well, then, where's the Great Sahara? In England or in Scotland?"

"'Tain't in either; it's in Africa."

Jim's eyes bugged out, and he begun to stare down with no end of interest, because that was where his originals come from; but I didn't more than half believe it. I couldn't, you know; it seemed too awful far away for us to have traveled.

But Tom was full of his discovery, as he called it,

46

hadn't dropped the glass and begun to clap his hands like a maniac and sing out:

"Camels!—Camels!"

So I grabbed a glass and Jim, too, and took a look, but I was disappointed, and says:

"Camels your granny; they're spiders."

"Spiders in a desert, you shad? Spiders walking in a procession? You don't ever reflect, Huck Finn, and I reckon you really haven't got anything to reflect *with*. Don't you know we're as much as a mile up in the air, and that that string of crawlers is two or three miles away? Spiders, good land! Spiders as big as a cow? Perhaps you'd like to go down and milk one of 'em. But they're camels, just the same. It's a caravan, that's what it is, and it's a mile long."

"Well, then, let's go down and look at it. I don't believe in it, and ain't going to till I see it and know it."

"All right," he says, and give the command: "Lower away."

As we come slanting down into the hot weather, we could see that it was camels, sure enough, plodding along, an everlasting string of them, with bales strapped to them, and several hundred men in long white robes, and a thing like a shawl bound over their heads and hanging down with tassels and fringes; and some of the men had long guns and some hadn't, and some was riding and some was walking. And the weather — well, it was just roasting. And how slow they did creep along! We swooped down now, all of a sudden, and stopped about a hundred yards over their heads.

The men all set up a yell, and some of them fell flat on their stomachs, some begun to fire their guns at us, and the rest broke and scampered every which way, and so did the camels.

We see that we was making trouble, so we went up again about a mile, to the cool weather, and watched them from there. It took them an hour to get together and form the procession again; then they started along, but we could see by the glasses that they wasn't paying much attention to anything but us. We poked along, looking down at them with the glasses, and by and by we see a big sand mound, and something like people the other side of it, and there was something like a man laying on top of the mound that raised his head up every now and then, and seemed to be watching the caravan or us, we didn't know which. As the caravan got nearer, he sneaked down on the other side and rushed to the other men and horses—for that is what they was—and we see them mount in a hurry; and next, here they come, like a house afire, some with lances and some with long guns, and all of them yelling the best they could.

They come a-tearing down onto the caravan, and the next minute both sides crashed together and was all mixed up, and there was such another popping of guns as you never heard, and the air got so full of smoke you could only catch glimpses of them struggling together. There must 'a' been six hundred men in that battle, and it was terrible to see. Then they broke up into gangs and groups, fighting tooth and nail, and scurrying and scampering around, and laying into each other like everything; and whenever the smoke cleared a little you could see dead and wounded people and camels scattered far and wide and all about, and camels racing off in every direction.

At last the robbers see they couldn't win, so their chief sounded a signal, and all that was left of them broke away and went scampering across the plain. The last man to go snatched up a child and carried it off in front of him on his horse, and a woman run screaming and begging after him, and followed him away off across the plain till she was separated a long ways from her people; but it warn't no use, and she had to give it up, and we see her sink down on the sand and cover her face with her hands. Then Tom took the hellum, and started for that yahoo, and we come a-whizzing down and made a swoop, and knocked him out of the saddle, child and all; and he was jarred considerable, but the child wasn't hurt, but laid there working its hands and legs in the air like a tumble-bug that's on its back and can't turn over. The man went staggering off to overtake his horse, and didn't know what had hit him, for we was three or four hundred yards up in the air by this time.

We judged the woman would go and get the child now; but she didn't. We could see her, through the glass, still setting there, with her head bowed down on her knees; so of course she hadn't seen the performance, and thought her child was clean gone with the man. She was nearly a half a mile from her people, so we thought we might go down to the child, which was about a quarter of a mile beyond

her, and snake it to her before the caravan people
could git to us to do us any harm; and besides, we
reckoned they had enough business on their hands
for one while, anyway, with the wounded. We
thought we'd chance it, and we did. We swooped
down and stopped, and Jim shinned down the ladder
and fetched up the kid, which was a nice fat little
thing, and in a noble good humor, too, considering
it was just out of a battle and been tumbled off of
a horse; and then we started for the mother, and
stopped back of her and tolerable near by, and Jim
slipped down and crept up easy, and when he was
close back of her the child goo-goo'd, the way a child
does, and she heard it, and whirled and fetched a
shriek of joy, and made a jump for the kid and
snatched it and hugged it, and dropped it and hugged
Jim, and then snatched off a gold chain and hung it
around Jim's neck, and hugged him again, and jerked
up the child again, a-sobbing and glorifying all the
time; and Jim he shoved for the ladder and up it,
and in a minute we was back up in the sky and the
woman was staring up, with the back of her head
between her shoulders and the child with its arms
locked around her neck. And there she stood, as
long as we was in sight a-sailing away in the sky.

CHAPTER VII

TOM RESPECTS THE FLEA

"NOON!" says Tom, and so it was. His shadder was just a blot around his feet. We looked, and the Grinnage clock was so close to twelve the difference didn't amount to nothing. So Tom said London was right north of us or right south of us, one or t'other, and he reckoned by the weather and the sand and the camels it was north; and a good many miles north, too; as many as from New York to the city of Mexico, he guessed.

Jim said he reckoned a balloon was a good deal the fastest thing in the world, unless it might be some kinds of birds—a wild pigeon, maybe, or a railroad.

But Tom said he had read about railroads in England going nearly a hundred miles an hour for a little ways, and there never was a bird in the world that could do that—except one, and that was a flea.

"A flea? Why, Mars Tom, in de fust place he ain't a bird, strickly speakin'—"

"He ain't a bird, eh? Well, then, what is he?"

"I don't rightly know, Mars Tom, but I speck he's only jist a' animal. No, I reckon dat won't do, nuther, he ain't big enough for a' animal. He mus' be a bug. Yassir, dat's what he is, he's a bug."

53

"I bet he ain't, but let it go. What's your second place?"

"Well, in de second place, birds is creturs dat goes a long ways, but a flea don't."

"He don't, don't he? Come, now, what *is* a long distance, if you know?"

"Why, it's miles, and lots of 'em—anybody knows dat."

"Can't a man walk miles?"

"Yassir, he kin."

"As many as a railroad?"

"Yassir, if you give him time."

"Can't a flea?"

"Well—I s'pose so—ef you gives him heaps of time."

"Now you begin to see, don't you, that *distance* ain't the thing to judge by, at all; it's the time it takes to go the distance *in* that *counts*, ain't it?"

"Well, hit do look sorter so, but I wouldn't 'a' b'lieved it, Mars Tom."

"It's a matter of *proportion*, that's what it is; and when you come to gauge a thing's speed by its size, where's your bird and your man and your railroad 'longside of a flea? The fastest man can't run more than about ten miles in an hour—not much over ten thousand times his own length. But all the books says any common ordinary third-class flea can jump a hundred and fifty times his own length; yes, and he can make five jumps a second too—seven hundred and fifty times his own length, in one little second— for he don't fool away any time stopping and starting —he does them both at the same time; you'll see,

54

if you try to put your finger on him. Now that's a common, ordinary, third-class flea's gait; but you take an Eyetalian *first*-class, that's been the pet of the nobility all his life, and hasn't ever knowed what want or sickness or exposure was, and he can jump more than three hundred times his own length, and keep it up all day, five such jumps every second, which is fifteen hundred times his own length. Well, suppose a man could go fifteen hundred times his own length in a second—say, a mile and a half. It's ninety miles a minute; it's considerable more than five thousand miles an hour. Where's your man *now?*—yes, and your bird, and your railroad, and your balloon? Laws, they don't amount to shucks 'longside of a flea. A flea is just a comet b'iled down small."

Jim was a good deal astonished, and so was I. Jim said:

"Is dem figgers jist edjackly true, en no jokin' en no lies, Mars Tom?"

"Yes, they are; they're perfectly true."

"Well, den, honey, a body's got to respec' a flea. I ain't had no respec' for um befo', sca'sely, but dey ain't no gittin' roun' it, dey do deserve it, dat's certain."

"Well, I bet they do. They've got ever so much more sense, and brains, and brightness, in proportion to their size, than any other cretur in the world. A person can learn them 'most anything; and they learn it quicker than any other cretur, too. They've been learnt to haul little carriages in harness, and go this way and that way and t'other way according to their orders; yes, and to march and drill like soldiers, doing it as exact, according to orders, as soldiers does it. They've been learnt to do all sorts of hard and troublesome things. S'pose you could cultivate a flea up to the size of a man, and keep his natural smartness a-growing and a-growing right along up, bigger and bigger, and keener and keener, in the same proportion—where'd the human race be, do you reckon? That flea would be President of the United States, and you couldn't any more prevent it than you can prevent lightning."

"My lan', Mars Tom, I never knowed dey was so much *to* de beas'. No, sir, I never had no idea of it, and dat's de fac'."

"There's more to him, by a long sight, than there is to any other cretur, man or beast, in proportion to size. He's the interestingest of them all. People have so much to say about an ant's strength, and an elephant's, and a locomotive's. Shucks, they don't begin with a flea. He can lift two or three hundred times his own weight. And none of them can come anywhere near it. And, moreover, he has got notions of his own, and is very particular, and you can't fool him; his instinct, or his judgment, or whatever it is, is perfectly sound and clear, and don't ever make a mistake. People think all humans are alike to a flea. It ain't so. There's folks that he won't go near, hungry or not hungry, and I'm one of them. I've never had one of them on me in my life."

"Mars Tom!"

"It's so; I ain't joking."

"Well, sah, I hain't ever heard de likes o' dat befo'."

Jim couldn't believe it, and I couldn't; so we had to drop down to the sand and git a supply and see. Tom was right. They went for me and Jim by the thousand, but not a one of them lit on Tom. There warn't no explaining it, but there it was and there warn't no getting around it. He said it had always been just so, and he'd just as soon be where there was a million of them as not; they'd never touch him nor bother him.

We went up to the cold weather to freeze 'em out, and stayed a little spell, and then come back to the comfortable weather and went lazying along twenty or twenty-five miles an hour, the way we'd been doing for the last few hours. The reason was, that the longer we was in that solemn, peaceful desert, the more the hurry and fuss got kind of soothed down in us, and the more happier and contented and satisfied we got to feeling, and the more we got to liking the desert, and then loving it. So we had cramped the speed down, as I was saying, and was having a most noble good lazy time, sometimes watching through the glasses, sometimes stretched out on the lockers reading, sometimes taking a nap.

It didn't seem like we was the same lot that was in such a state to find land and git ashore, but it was. But we had got over that—clean over it. We was used to the balloon now and not afraid any more, and didn't want to be anywheres else. Why, it seemed just like home; it 'most seemed as if I had been born and raised in it, and Jim and Tom said the same. And always I had had hateful people around me, a-nagging at me, and pestering of me, and scolding, and finding fault, and fussing and bothering, and sticking to me, and keeping after me, and making me do this, and making me do that and t'other, and always selecting out the things I didn't want to do, and then giving me Sam Hill because I shirked and done something else, and just aggravating the life out of a body all the time; but up here in the sky it was so still and sunshiny and lovely, and plenty to eat, and plenty of sleep, and strange things to see, and no nagging and no pestering, and no good people, and just holiday all the time. Land, I warn't in no hurry to git out and buck at civilization again. Now, one of the worst things about civilization is, that anybody that gits a letter with trouble in it comes and tells you all about it and makes you feel bad, and the newspapers fetches you the troubles of everybody all over the world, and keeps you downhearted and dismal 'most all the time, and it's such a heavy load for a person. I hate them newspapers; and I hate letters; and if I had my way I wouldn't allow nobody to load his troubles onto other folks he ain't acquainted with, on t'other side of the world, that way. Well, up in a balloon there ain't any of that, and it's the darlingest place there is.

We had supper, and that night was one of the prettiest nights I ever see. The moon made it just like daylight, only a heap softer; and once we see a lion standing all alone by himself, just all alone on the earth, it seemed like, and his shadder laid on the sand by him like a puddle of ink. That's the kind of moonlight to have.

Mainly we laid on our backs and talked; we didn't want to go to sleep. Tom said we was right in the midst of the *Arabian Nights* now. He said it was right along here that one of the cutest things in that book happened; so we looked down and watched while he told about it, because there ain't anything that is so interesting to look at as a place that a book has talked about. It was a tale about a camel-driver that had lost his camel, and he come along in the desert and met a man, and says:

"Have you run across a stray camel to-day?"

And the man says:

"Was he blind in his left eye?"

"Yes."

"Had he lost an upper front tooth?"

"Yes."

"Was his off hind leg lame?"

"Yes."

"Was he loaded with millet-seed on one side and honey on the other?"

"Yes, but you needn't go into no more details— that's the one, and I'm in a hurry. Where did you see him?"

"I hain't seen him at all," the man says.

"Hain't seen him at all? How can you describe him so close, then?"

"Because when a person knows how to use his eyes, everything has got a meaning to it; but most people's eyes ain't any good to them. I knowed a camel had been along, because I seen his track. I knowed he was lame in his off hind leg because he had favored that foot and trod light on it, and his track showed it. I knowed he was blind on his left side because he only nibbled the grass on the right side of the trail. I knowed he had lost an upper front tooth because where he bit into the sod his teeth-print showed it. The millet-seed sifted out on one side—the ants told me that; the honey leaked out on the other—the flies told me that. I know all about your camel, but I hain't seen him."

Jim says:

"Go on, Mars Tom, hit's a mighty good tale, and powerful interestin'."

"That's all," Tom says.

"*All?*" says Jim, astonished. "What 'come o' de camel?"

"I don't know."

"Mars Tom, don't de tale say?"

"No."

Jim puzzled a minute, then he says:

"Well! Ef dat ain't de beatenes' tale ever *I* struck. Jist gits to de place whah de intrust is gittin' red-hot, en down she breaks. Why, Mars Tom, dey ain't no *sense* in a tale dat acts like dat. Hain't you got no *idea* whether de man got de camel back er not?"

"No, I haven't."

I see myself there warn't no sense in the tale, to chop square off that way before it come to anything, but I warn't going to say so, because I could see Tom was souring up pretty fast over the way it flatted out and the way Jim had popped onto the weak place in it, and I don't think it's fair for everybody to pile onto a feller when he's down. But Tom he whirls on me and says:

"What do *you* think of the tale?"

Of course, then, I had to come out and make a clean breast and say it did seem to me, too, same as it did to Jim, that as long as the tale stopped square in the middle and never got to no place, it really warn't worth the trouble of telling.

Tom's chin dropped on his breast, and 'stead of being mad, as I reckoned he'd be, to hear me scoff at his tale that way, he seemed to be only sad; and he says:

"Some people can see, and some can't—just as that man said. Let alone a camel, if a cyclone had gone by, *you* duffers wouldn't 'a' noticed the track."

I don't know what he meant by that, and he didn't say; it was just one of his irrulevances, I reckon—he was full of them, sometimes, when he was in a close place and couldn't see no other way out—but I didn't mind. We'd spotted the soft place in that tale sharp enough, he couldn't git away from that little fact. It graveled him like the nation, too, I reckon, much as he tried not to let on.

CHAPTER VIII

THE DISAPPEARING LAKE

WE had an early breakfast in the morning, and set looking down on the desert, and the weather was ever so bammy and lovely, although we warn't high up. You have to come down lower and lower after sundown in the desert, because it cools off so fast; and so, by the time it is getting toward dawn, you are skimming along only a little ways above the sand.

We was watching the shadder of the balloon slide along the ground, and now and then gazing off across the desert to see if anything was stirring, and then down on the shadder again, when all of a sudden almost right under us we see a lot of men and camels laying scattered about, perfectly quiet, like they was asleep.

We shut off the power, and backed up and stood over them, and then we see that they was all dead. It give us the cold shivers. And it made us hush down, too, and talk low, like people at a funeral. We dropped down slow and stopped, and me and Tom clumb down and went among them. There was men, and women, and children. They was dried by the sun, and dark and shriveled and leathery, like the pictures of mummies you see in books. And yet they looked just as human, you wouldn't 'a' believed it; just like they was asleep.

Some of the people and animals was partly covered with sand, but most of them not, for the sand was thin there, and the bed was gravel and hard. Most of the clothes had rotted away; and when you took hold of a rag, it tore with a touch, like spider-web. Tom reckoned they had been laying there for years.

Some of the men had rusty guns by them, some had swords on and had shawl belts with long, silver-mounted pistols stuck in them. All the camels had their loads on yet, but the packs had busted or rotted and spilt the freight out on the ground. We didn't reckon the swords was any good to the dead people any more, so we took one apiece, and some pistols. We took a small box, too, because it was so handsome and inlaid so fine; and then we wanted to bury the people; but there warn't no way to do it that we could think of, and nothing to do it with but sand, and that would blow away again, of course.

Then we mounted high and sailed away, and pretty soon that black spot on the sand was out of sight, and we wouldn't ever see them poor people again in this world. We wondered, and reasoned, and tried to guess how they come to be there, and how it all happened to them, but we couldn't make it out. First we thought maybe they got lost, and wandered around and about till their food and water give out and they starved to death; but Tom said no wild animals nor vultures hadn't meddled with them, and so that guess wouldn't do. So at last we give it up, and judged we wouldn't think about it no more, because it made us low-spirited.

Then we opened the box, and it had gems and jewels in it, quite a pile, and some little veils of the kind the dead women had on, with fringes made out of curious gold money that we warn't acquainted with. We wondered if we better go and try to find them again and give it back; but Tom thought it over and said no, it was a country that was full of robbers, and they would come and steal it; and then the sin would be on us for putting the temptation in their way. So we went on; but I wished we had took all they had, so there wouldn't 'a' been no temptation at all left.

We had had two hours of that blazing weather down there, and was dreadful thirsty when we got aboard again. We went straight for the water, but it was spoiled and bitter, besides being pretty near hot enough to scald your mouth. We couldn't drink it. It was Mississippi River water, the best in the world, and we stirred up the mud in it to see if that would help, but no, the mud wasn't any better than the water.

Well, we hadn't been so very, very thirsty before, while we was interested in the lost people, but we was now, and as soon as we found we couldn't have a drink, we was more than thirty-five times as thirsty as we was a quarter of a minute before. Why, in a little while we wanted to hold our mouths open and pant like a dog.

Tom said to keep a sharp lookout, all around, everywheres, because we'd got to find an oasis or

there warn't no telling what would happen. So we
done it. We kept the glasses gliding around all the
time, till our arms got so tired we couldn't hold them
any more. Two hours—three hours—just gazing
and gazing, and nothing but sand, sand, *sand*, and
you could see the quivering heat-shimmer playing
over it. Dear, dear, a body don't know what real
misery is till he is thirsty all the way through and is
certain he ain't ever going to come to any water any
more. At last I couldn't stand it to look around on
them baking plains; I laid down on the locker, and
give it up.

But by and by Tom raised a whoop, and there she
was! A lake, wide and shiny, with pa'm trees lean-
ing over it asleep, and their shadders in the water
just as soft and delicate as ever you see. I never see
anything look so good. It was a long ways off, but
that warn't anything to us; we just slapped on a
hundred-mile gait, and calculated to be there in seven
minutes; but she stayed the same old distance away,
all the time; we couldn't seem to gain on her; yes,
sir, just as far, and shiny, and like a dream; but we
couldn't get no nearer; and at last, all of a sudden,
she was gone!

Tom's eyes took a spread, and he says:

"Boys, it was a *my*ridge!" Said it like he was
glad. I didn't see nothing to be glad about. I says:

"Maybe. I don't care nothing about its name, the
thing I want to know is, what's become of it?"

Jim was trembling all over, and so scared he
couldn't speak, but he wanted to ask that question
himself if he could 'a' done it. Tom says:

"What's *become* of it? Why, you see yourself **it's** gone."

"Yes, I know; but where's it gone *to?*"

He looked me over and says:

"Well, now, Huck Finn, where *would* it go to! Don't you know what a myridge is?"

"No, I don't. What is it?"

"It ain't anything but imagination. There ain't anything *to* it."

It warmed me up a little to hear him talk like that, and I says:

"What's the use you talking that kind of stuff, Tom Sawyer? Didn't I see the lake?"

"Yes—you think you did."

"I don't think nothing about it, I *did* see it."

"I tell you you *didn't* see it either—because it warn't there to see."

It astonished Jim to hear him talk so, and he broke in and says, kind of pleading and distressed:

"Mars Tom, *please* don't say sich things in sich an awful time as dis. You ain't only reskin' yo' own self, but you's reskin' us—same way like Anna Nias en Siffira. De lake *wuz* dah—I seen it jis' as plain as I sees you en Huck dis minute."

I says:

"Why, he seen it himself! He was the very one that seen it first. *Now*, then!"

"Yes, Mars Tom, hit's so—you can't deny it. We all seen it, en dat *prove* it was dah."

"Proves it! *How* does it prove it?"

"Same way it does in de courts en everywheres, Mars Tom. One pusson might be drunk, or dreamy, or suthin', en he could be mistaken; en two might, maybe; but I tell you, sah, when three sees a thing, drunk er sober, it's *so*. Dey ain't no gittin' aroun' dat, en you knows it, Mars Tom.''

"I don't know nothing of the kind. There used to be forty thousand million people that seen the sun move from one side of the sky to the other every day. Did that prove that the sun *done* it?"

"'Course it did. En besides, dey warn't no 'casion to prove it. A body 'at's got any sense ain't gwine to doubt it. Dah she is now—a-sailin' thoo de sky, like she allays done."

Tom turned on me, then, and says:

"What do *you* say—is the sun standing still?"

"Tom Sawyer, what's the use to ask such a jack-ass question? Anybody that ain't blind can see it don't stand still."

"Well," he says, "I'm lost in the sky with no company but a passel of low-down animals that don't know no more than the head boss of a university did three or four hundred years ago."

It warn't fair play, and I let him know it. I says:

"Throwin' mud ain't arguin', Tom Sawyer."

"Oh, my goodness, oh, my goodness gracious, dah't de lake ag'in!" yelled Jim, just then. "*Now*, Mars Tom, what you gwine to say?"

Yes, sir, there was the lake again, away yonder across the desert, perfectly plain, trees and all, just the same as it was before. I says:

"I reckon you're satisfied now, Tom Sawyer."

But he says, perfectly ca'm:

"Yes, satisfied there ain't no lake there."

Jim says:

"*Don't* talk so, Mars Tom—it sk'yers me to hear you. It's so hot, en you's so thirsty, dat you ain't in yo' right mine, Mars Tom. Oh, but don't she look good! 'clah I doan' know how I's gwine to wait tell we gits dah, I's *so* thirsty."

"Well, you'll have to wait; and it won't do you no good, either, because there ain't no lake there, I tell you."

I says:

"Jim, don't you take your eye off of it, and I won't, either."

"'Deed I won't; en bless you, honey, I couldn't ef I wanted to."

We went a-tearing along toward it, piling the miles behind us like nothing, but never gaining an inch on it—and all of a sudden it was gone again! Jim staggered, and 'most fell down. When he got his breath he says, gasping like a fish:

"Mars Tom, hit's a *ghos'*, dat's what it is, en I hopes to goodness we ain't gwine to see it no mo'. Dey's *been* a lake, en suthin's happened, en de lake's dead, en we's seen its ghos'; we's seen it twiste, en dat's proof. De desert's ha'nted, it's ha'nted, sho; oh, Mars Tom, le's git outen it; I'd ruther die den have de night ketch us in it ag'in en de ghos' er dat lake come a-mournin' aroun' us en we asleep en doan' know de danger we's in."

"Ghost, you gander! It ain't anything but air and heat and thirstiness pasted together by a person's imagination. If I—gimme the glass!"

He grabbed it and begun to gaze off to the right.

"It's a flock of birds," he says. "It's getting toward sundown, and they're making a bee-line across our track for somewheres. They mean business—maybe they're going for food or water, or both. Let her go to starboard!—Port your hellum! Hard down! There—ease up—steady, as you go."

We shut down some of the power, so as not to outspeed them, and took out after them. We went skimming along a quarter of a mile behind them, and when we had followed them an hour and a half and was getting pretty discouraged, and was thirsty clean to unendurableness, Tom says:

"Take the glass, one of you, and see what that is, away ahead of the birds."

Jim got the first glimpse, and slumped down on the locker sick. He was most crying, and says:

"She's dah ag'in, Mars Tom, she's dah ag'in, en I knows I's gwine to die, 'case when a body sees a ghos' de third time, dat's what it means. I wisht I'd never come in dis balloon, dat I does."

He wouldn't look no more, and what he said made me afraid, too, because I knowed it was true, for that has always been the way with ghosts; so then I wouldn't look any more, either. Both of us begged Tom to turn off and go some other way, but he wouldn't, and said we was ignorant superstitious blatherskites. Yes, and he'll git come up with, one of these days, I says to myself, insulting ghosts that way. They'll stand it for a while, maybe, but they won't stand it always, for anybody that knows about ghosts knows how easy they are hurt, and how revengeful they are.

So we was all quiet and still, Jim and me being scared, and Tom busy. By and by Tom fetched the balloon to a standstill, and says:

"*Now* get up and look, you sapheads."

We done it, and there was the sure-enough water right under us!—clear, and blue, and cool, and deep, and wavy with the breeze, the loveliest sight that ever was. And all about it was grassy banks, and flowers, and shady groves of big trees, looped together with vines, and all looking so peaceful and comfortable—enough to make a body cry, it was so beautiful.

Jim *did* cry, and rip and dance and carry on, he was so thankful and out of his mind for joy. It was my watch, so I had to stay by the works, but Tom and Jim clumb down and drunk a barrel apiece, and fetched me up a lot, and I've tasted a many a good thing in my life, but nothing that ever begun with that water.

Then we went down and had a swim, and then Tom came up and spelled me, and me and Jim had a swim, and then Jim spelled Tom, and me and Tom had a foot-race and a boxing-mill, and I don't reckon I ever had such a good time in my life. It warn't so very hot, because it was close on to evening, and we hadn't any clothes on, anyway. Clothes is well enough in school, and in towns, and at balls, too, but there ain't no sense in them when there ain't no civilization nor other kinds of bothers and fussiness around.

"Lions a-comin'!—lions! Quick, Mars Tom! Jump for yo' life, Huck!"

Oh, and didn't we! We never stopped for clothes, but waltzed up the ladder just so. Jim lost his head straight off—he always done it whenever he got excited and scared; and so now, 'stead of just easing the ladder up from the ground a little, so the animals couldn't reach it, he turned on a raft of power, and we went whizzing up and was dangling in the sky before he got his wits together and seen what a foolish thing he was doing. Then he stopped her, but he had clean forgot what to do next; so there we was, so high that the lions looked like pups, and we was drifting off on the wind.

But Tom he shinned up and went for the works and begun to slant her down, and back toward the lake, where the animals was gathering like a camp-meeting, and I judged he had lost *his* head, too; for he knowed I was too scared to climb, and did he want to dump me among the tigers and things?

But no, his head was level; he knowed what he was about. He swooped down to within thirty or forty feet of the lake, and stopped right over the center, and sung out:

"Leggo, and drop!"

I done it, and shot down, feet first, and seemed to go about a mile toward the bottom; and when I come up, he says:

"Now lay on your back and float till you're rested and got your pluck back, then I'll dip the ladder in the water and you can climb aboard."

I done it. Now that was ever so smart in Tom, because if he had started off somewheres else to drop down on the sand, the menagerie would 'a' come along, too, and might 'a' kept us hunting a safe place till I got tuckered out and fell.

And all this time the lions and tigers was sorting

out the clothes, and trying to divide them up so there would be some for all, but there was a misunderstanding about it somewheres, on account of some of them trying to hog more than their share; so there was another insurrection, and you never see anything like it in the world. There must 'a' been fifty of them, all mixed up together, snorting and roaring and snapping and biting and tearing, legs and tails in the air, and you couldn't tell which was which, and the sand and fur a-flying. And when they got done, some was dead, and some was limping off crippled, and the rest was setting around on the battle-field, some of them licking their sore places and the others looking up at us and seemed to be kind of inviting us to come down and have some fun, but which we didn't want any.

As for the clothes, they warn't any, any more. Every last rag of them was inside of the animals; and not agreeing with them very well, I don't reckon, for there was considerable many brass buttons on them, and there was knives in the pockets, too, and smoking-tobacco, and nails and chalk and marbles and fish-hooks and things. But I wasn't caring. All that was bothering me was, that all we had now was the professor's clothes, a big enough assortment, but not suitable to go into company with, if we came across any, because the britches was as long as tunnels, and the coats and things according. Still, there was everything a tailor needed, and Jim was a kind of jack-legged tailor, and he allowed he could soon trim a suit or two down for us that would answer.

CHAPTER IX

TOM DISCOURSES ON THE DESERT

STILL, we thought we would drop down there a minute, but on another errand. Most of the professor's cargo of food was put up in cans, in the new way that somebody had just invented; the rest was fresh. When you fetch Missouri beefsteak to the Great Sahara, you want to be particular and stay up in the coolish weather. So we reckoned we would drop down into the lion market and see how we could make out there.

We hauled in the ladder and dr pped down till we was just above the reach of the animals, then we let down a rope with a slip-knot in it and hauled up a dead lion, a small tender one, then yanked up a cub tiger. We had to keep the congregation off with the revolver, or they would 'a' took a hand in the proceedings and helped.

We carved off a supply from both, and saved the skins, and hove the rest overboard. Then we baited some of the professor's hooks with the fresh meat and went a-fishing. We stood over the lake just a convenient distance above the water, and catched a lot of the nicest fish you ever see. It was a most amazing good supper we had; lion steak, tiger steak, fried fish, and hot corn-pone. I don't want nothing better than that.

We had some fruit to finish off with. We got it out of the top of a monstrous tall tree. It was a very slim tree that hadn't a branch on it from the bottom plumb to the top, and there it bursted out like a feather duster. It was a pa'm tree, of course; anybody knows a pa'm tree the minute he see it, by the pictures. We went for cocoanuts in this one, but there warn't none. There was only big loose bunches of things like oversized grapes, and Tom allowed they was dates, because he said they answered the description in the *Arabian Nights* and the other books. Of course they mightn't be, and they might be poison; so we had to wait a spell, and watch and see if the birds et them. They done it; so we done it, too, and they was most amazing good.

By this time monstrous big birds begun to come and settle on the dead animals. They was plucky creturs; they would tackle one end of a lion that was being gnawed at the other end by another lion. If the lion drove the bird away, it didn't do no good; he was back again the minute the lion was busy.

The big birds come out of every part of the sky —you could make them out with the glass while they was still so far away you couldn't see them with your naked eye. Tom said the birds didn't find out the meat was there by the smell; they had to find it out by seeing it. Oh, but ain't that an eye for you! Tom said at the distance of five mile a patch of dead lions couldn't look any bigger than a person's finger-nail, and he couldn't imagine how the birds could notice such a little thing so far off.

It was strange and unnatural to see lion eat lion,

and we thought maybe they warn't kin. But Jim
said that didn't make no difference. He said a hog
was fond of her own children, and so was a spider,
and he reckoned maybe a lion was pretty near as
unprincipled, though maybe not quite. He thought
likely a lion wouldn't eat his own father, if he knowed
which was him, but reckoned he would eat his
brother-in-law if he was uncommon hungry, and
eat his mother-in-law any time. But *reckoning*
don't settle nothing. You can reckon till the cows
come home, but that don't fetch you to no decision.
So we give it up and let it drop.

Generly it was very still in the desert nights, but
this time there was music. A lot of other animals
come to dinner; sneaking yelpers that Tom allowed
was jackals, and roached-backed ones that he said
was hyenas; and all the whole biling of them kept
up a racket all the time. They made a picture in
the moonlight that was more different than any
picture I ever see. We had a line out and made
fast to the top of a tree, and didn't stand no watch,
but all turned in and slept; but I was up two or
three times to look down at the animals and hear
the music. It was like having a front seat at a
menagerie for nothing, which I hadn't ever had before, and so it seemed foolish to sleep and not make
the most of it; I mightn't ever have such a chance
again.

We went a-fishing again in the early dawn, and
then lazied around all day in the deep shade on an
island, taking turn about to watch and see that
none of the animals come a-snooping around there

after erronorts for dinner. We was going to leave the next day, but couldn't, it was too lovely.

The day after, when we rose up toward the sky and sailed off eastward, we looked back and watched that place till it warn't nothing but just a speck in the desert, and I tell you it was like saying good-by to a friend that you ain't ever going to see any more.

Jim was thinking to himself, and at last he says:

"Mars Tom, we's mos' to de end er de desert now, I speck."

"Why?"

"Well, hit stan' to reason we is. You knows how long we's been a-skimmin' over it. Mus' be mos' out o' san'. Hit's a wonder to me dat it's hilt out as long as it has."

"Shucks, there's plenty sand, you needn't worry."

"Oh, I ain't a-worryin', Mars Tom, only wonder-in', dat's all. De Lord's got plenty san', I ain't doubtin' dat; but nemmine, He ain't gwyne to *was'e* it jist on dat account; en I allows dat dis desert's plenty big enough now, jist de way she is, en you can't spread her out no mo' 'dout was'in' san'."

"Oh, go 'long! we ain't much more than fairly *started* across this desert yet. The United States is a pretty big country, ain't it? Ain't it, Huck?"

"Yes," I says, "there ain't no bigger one, I don't reckon."

"Well," he says, "this desert is about the shape of the United States, and if you was to lay it down on top of the United States, it would cover the land of the free out of sight like a blanket. There'd be a little corner sticking out, up at Maine and away up northwest, and Florida sticking out like a turtle's tail, and that's all. We've took California away from the Mexicans two or three years ago, so that part of the Pacific coast is ours now, and if you laid the Great Sahara down with her edge on the Pacific, she would cover the United States and stick out past New York six hundred miles into the Atlantic Ocean."

I says:

"Good land! have you got the documents for that, Tom Sawyer?"

"Yes, and they're right here, and I've been studying them. You can look for yourself. From New York to the Pacific is 2,600 miles. From one end of the Great Desert to the other is 3,200. The United States contains 3,600,000 square miles, the desert contains 4,162,000. With the desert's bulk you could cover up every last inch of the United States, and in under, where the edges projected out, you could tuck England, Scotland, Ireland, France, Denmark, and all Germany. Yes, sir, you could hide the home of the brave and all of them countries clean out of sight under the Great Sahara, and you would still have 2,000 square miles of sand left."

"Well," I says, "it clean beats me. Why, Tom, it shows that the Lord took as much pains makin' this desert as makin' the United States and all them other countries."

Jim says: "Huck, dat don' stan' to reason. I reckon dis desert wa'n't made at all. Now you take en look at it like dis—you look at it, and see ef I's right. What's a desert good for? 'Tain't good

for nuthin'. Dey ain't no way to make **it pay.**
Hain't dat so, Huck?"

"Yes, I reckon."

"Hain't it so, Mars Tom?"

"I guess so. Go on."

"Ef a thing ain't no good, it's made **in vain, ain't**
it?"

"Yes."

"*Now*, den! Do de Lord make anything **in vain?**
You answer me dat."

"Well—no, He don't."

"Den how come He make a desert?"

"Well, go on. How *did* He come to make it?"

"Mars Tom, *I* b'lieve it uz jes like when **you's**
buildin' a house; dey's allays a lot o' truck en rubbish lef' over. What does you do wid it? Doan'
you take en k'yart if off en dump it into a ole vacant
back lot? 'Course. Now, den, it's my opinion hit
was jest like dat—dat de Great Sahara warn't made
at all, she jes' *happen*'."

I said it was a real good argument, and I believed
it was the best one Jim ever made. Tom he said
the same, but said the trouble about arguments is,
they ain't nothing but *theories*, after all, and theories
don't prove nothing, they only give you a place to
rest on, a spell, when you are tuckered out butting
around and around trying to find out something
there ain't no way *to* find out. And he says:

"There's another trouble about theories: there's
always a hole in them somewheres, sure, if you look
close enough. It's just so with this one of Jim's.
Look what billions and billions of stars there **is.**

How does it come that there was just exactly enough star-stuff, and none left over? How does it come there ain't no sand-pile up there?"

But Jim was fixed for him and says:

"What's de Milky Way?—dat's what *I* want to know. What's de Milky Way? Answer me dat!"

In my opinion it was just a sockdologer. It's only an opinion, it's only *my* opinion and others may think different; but I said it then and I stand to it now—it was a sockdologer. And moreover, besides, it landed Tom Sawyer. He couldn't say a word. He had that stunned look of a person that's been shot in the back with a kag of nails. All he said was, as for people like me and Jim, he'd just as soon have intellectual intercourse with a catfish. But anybody can say that—and I notice they always do when somebody has fetched them a lifter. Tom Sawyer was tired of that end of the subject.

So we got back to talking about the size of the desert again, and the more we compared it with this and that and t'other thing, the more nobler and bigger and grander it got to look right along. And so, hunting among the figgers, Tom found, by and by, that it was just the same size as the Empire of China. Then he showed us the spread the Empire of China made on the map, and the room she took up in the world. Well, it was wonderful to think of, and I says:

"Why, I've heard talk about this desert plenty of times, but *I* never knowed before how important she was."

Then Tom says:

"Important! Sahara important! That's just the way with some people. If a thing's big, it's important. That's all the sense they've got. All they can see is *size*. Why, look at England. It's the most important country in the world; and yet you could put it in China's vest-pocket; and not only that, but you'd have the dickens's own time to find it again the next time you wanted it. And look at Russia. It spreads all around and everywhere, and yet ain't no more important in this world than Rhode Island is, and hasn't got half as much in it that's worth saving."

Away off now we see a little hill, a-standing up just on the edge of the world. Tom broke off his talk, and reached for a glass very much excited, and took a look, and says:

"That's it—it's the one I've been looking for, sure. If I'm right, it's the one the dervish took the man into and showed him all the treasures."

So we begun to gaze, and he begun to tell about it out of the *Arabian Nights*.

CHAPTER X

THE TREASURE-HILL

TOM said it happened like this:
A dervish was stumping it along through the desert, on foot, one blazing hot day, and he had come a thousand miles and was pretty poor, and hungry, and ornery and tired, and along about where we are now he run across a camel-driver with a hundred camels, and asked him for some a'ms. But the camel-driver he asked to be excused. The dervish said:

"Don't you own these camels?"

"Yes, they're mine."

"Are you in debt?"

"Who—me? No."

"Well, a man that owns a hundred camels and ain't in debt is rich—and not only rich, but very rich. Ain't it so?"

The camel-driver owned up that it was so. Then the dervish says:

"God has made you rich, and He has made me poor. He has His reasons, and they are wise, blessed be His name. But He has willed that His rich shall help His poor, and you have turned away from me, your brother, in my need, and He will remember this, and you will lose by it."

That made the camel-driver feel shaky, but all the same he was born hoggish after money and didn't like to let go a cent; so he begun to whine and explain, and said times was hard, and although he had took a full freight down to Balsora and got a fat rate for it, he couldn't git no return freight, and so he warn't making no great things out of his trip. So the dervish starts along again, and says:

"All right, if you want to take the risk; but I reckon you've made a mistake this time, and missed a chance."

Of course the camel-driver wanted to know what kind of a chance he had missed, because maybe there was money in it; so he run after the dervish, and begged him so hard and earnest to take pity on him that at last the dervish gave in, and says:

"Do you see that hill yonder? Well, in that hill is all the treasures of the earth, and I was looking around for a man with a particular good kind heart and a noble, generous disposition, because if I could find just that man, I've got a kind of a salve I could put on his eyes and he could see the treasures and get them out."

So then the camel-driver was in a sweat; and he cried, and begged, and took on, and went down on his knees, and said he was just that kind of a man, and said he could fetch a thousand people that would say he warn't ever described so exact before.

"Well, then," says the dervish, "all right. If we load the hundred camels, can I have half of them?"

The driver was so glad he couldn't hardly hold in, and says:

"Now you're shouting."

So they shook hands on the bargain, and the dervish got out his box and rubbed the salve on the driver's right eye, and the hill opened and he went in, and there, sure enough, was piles and piles of gold and jewels sparkling like all the stars in heaven had fell down.

So him and the dervish laid into it, and they loaded every camel till he couldn't carry no more; then they said good-by, and each of them started off with his fifty. But pretty soon the camel-driver come a-running and overtook the dervish and says:

"You ain't in society, you know, and you don't really need all you've got. Won't you be good, and let me have ten of your camels?"

"Well," the dervish says, "I don't know but what you say is reasonable enough."

So he done it, and they separated, and the dervish started off again with his forty. But pretty soon here comes the camel-driver bawling after him again, and whines and slobbers around and begs another ten off of him, saying thirty camel-loads of treasures was enough to see a dervish through, because they live very simple, you know, and don't keep house, but board around and give their note.

But that warn't the end yet. That ornery hound kept coming and coming till he had begged back all the camels and had the whole hundred. Then he was satisfied, and ever so grateful, and said he wouldn't ever forget the dervish as long as he lived, and nobody hadn't been so good to him before, and liberal. So they shook hands good-by, and separated and started off again.

But do you know, it warn't ten minutes till the camel-driver was unsatisfied again—he was the lowdownest reptyle in seven counties—and he come a-running again. And this time the thing he wanted was to get the dervish to rub some of the salve on his other eye.

"Why?" said the dervish.

"Oh, you know," says the driver.

"Know what?"

"Well, you can't fool me," says the driver. "You're trying to keep back something from me, you know it mighty well. You know, I reckon, that if I had the salve on the other eye I could see a lot more things that's valuable. Come—please put it on."

The dervish says:

"I wasn't keeping anything back from you. I don't mind telling you what would happen if I put it on. You'd never see again. You'd be stoneblind the rest of your days."

But do you know that beat wouldn't believe him. No, he begged and begged, and whined and cried, till at last the dervish opened his box and told him to put it on, if he wanted to. So the man done it, and, sure enough, he was as blind as a bat in a minute.

Then the dervish laughed at him and mocked at him and made fun of him; and says:

"Good-by—a man that's blind hain't got no use for jewelry."

And he cleared out with the hundred camels, and

left that man to wander around poor and miserable
and friendless the rest of his days in the desert.

Jim said he'd bet it was a lesson to him.

"Yes," Tom says, "and like a considerable many
lessons a body gets. They ain't no account, because
the thing don't ever happen the same way again—
and can't. The time Hen Scovil fell down the chim-
bly and crippled his back for life, everybody said it
would be a lesson to him. What kind of a lesson?
How was he going to use it? He couldn't climb
chimblies no more, and he hadn't no more backs to
break."

"All de same, Mars Tom, dey *is* sich a thing as
learnin' by expe'ence. De Good Book say de burnt
chile shun de fire."

"Well, I ain't denying that a thing's a lesson if
it's a thing that can happen twice just the same way.
There's lots of such things, and *they* educate a person,
that's what Uncle Abner always said; but there's
forty *million* lots of the other kind—the kind that
don't happen the same way twice—and they ain't
no real use, they ain't no more instructive than the
smallpox. When you've got it, it ain't no good to
find out you ought to been vaccinated, and it ain't
no good to git vaccinated afterward, because the
smallpox don't come but once. But, on the other
hand, Uncle Abner said that the person that had took
a bull by the tail once had learnt sixty or seventy
times as much as a person that hadn't, and said a
person that started in to carry a cat home by the tail
was gitting knowledge that was always going to be
useful to him, and warn't ever going to grow dim

or doubtful. But I can tell you, Jim, Uncle Abner was down on them people that's all the time trying to dig a lesson out of everything that happens, no matter whether—"

But Jim was asleep. Tom looked kind of ashamed, because you know a person always feels bad when he is talking uncommon fine and thinks the other person is admiring, and that other person goes to sleep that way. Of course he oughtn't to go to sleep, because it's shabby; but the finer a person talks the certainer it is to make you sleep, and so when you come to look at it it ain't nobody's fault in particular; both of them's to blame.

Jim begun to snore—soft and blubbery at first, then a long rasp, then a stronger one, then a half a dozen horrible ones, like the last water sucking down the plug-hole of a bath-tub, then the same with more power to it, and some big coughs and snorts flung in, the way a cow does that is choking to death; and when the person has got to that point he is at his level best, and can wake up a man that is in the next block with a dipperful of loddanum in him, but can't wake himself up although all that awful noise of his'n ain't but three inches from his own ears. And that is the curiousest thing in the world, seems to me. But you rake a match to light the candle, and that little bit of a noise will fetch him. I wish I knowed what was the reason of that, but there don't seem to be no way to find out. Now there was Jim alarming the whole desert, and yanking the animals out, for miles and miles around, to see what in the nation was going on up there; there warn't nobody nor nothing that was as close to the noise as *he* was, and yet he was the only cretur that wasn't disturbed by it. We yelled at him and whooped at him, it never done no good; but the first time there come a little wee noise that wasn't of a usual kind, it woke him up. No, sir, I've thought it all over, and so has Tom, and there ain't no way to find out why a snorer can't hear himself snore.

Jim said he hadn't been asleep; he just shut his eyes so he could listen better.

Tom said nobody warn't accusing him.

That made him look like he wished he hadn't said anything. And he wanted to git away from the subject, I reckon, because he begun to abuse the camel-driver, just the way a person does when he has got catched in something and wants to take it out of somebody else. He let into the camel-driver the hardest he knowed how, and I had to agree with him; and he praised up the dervish the highest he could, and I had to agree with him there, too. But Tom says:

"I ain't so sure. You call that dervish so dreadful liberal and good and unselfish, but I don't quite see it. He didn't hunt up another poor dervish, did he? No, he didn't. If he was so unselfish, why didn't he go in there himself and take a pocketful of jewels and go along and be satisfied? No, sir, the person he was hunting for was a man with a hundred camels. He wanted to get away with all the treasure he could."

"Why, Mars Tom, he was willin' to divide, fair and square; he only struck for fifty camels."

"Because he knowed how he was going to git all of them by and by."

"Mars Tom, he *tole* de man de truck would make him bline."

"Yes, because he knowed the man's character. It was just the kind of a man he was hunting for—a man that never believes in anybody's word or anybody's honorableness, because he ain't got none of his own. I reckon there's lots of people like that dervish. They swindle, right and left, but they always make the other person *seem* to swindle himself. They keep inside of the letter of the law all the time, and there ain't no way to git hold of them. *They* don't put the salve on—oh, no, that would be sin; but they know how to fool *you* into putting it on, then it's you that blinds yourself. I reckon the dervish and the camel-driver was just a pair—a fine, smart, brainy rascal, and a dull, coarse, ignorant one, but both of them rascals, just the same."

"Mars Tom, does you reckon dey's any o' dat kind o' salve in de worl' now?"

"Yes, Uncle Abner says there is. He says they've got it in New York, and they put it on country people's eyes and show them all the railroads in the world, and they go in and git them, and then when they rub the salve on the other eye the other man bids them good-by and goes off with their railroads. Here's the treasure-hill now. Lower away!"

We landed, but it warn't as interesting as I thought it was going to be, because we couldn't find the place where they went in to git the treasure. Still, it was plenty interesting enough, just to see the mere

hill itself where such a wonderful thing happened.
Jim said he wouldn't 'a' missed it for three dollars,
and I felt the same way.

And to me and Jim, as wonderful a thing as any
was the way Tom could come into a strange big
country like this and go straight and find a little
hump like that and tell it in a minute from a million
other humps that was almost just like it, and nothing to help him but only his own learning and his
own natural smartness. We talked and talked it
over together, but couldn't make out now he done
it. He had the best head on him I ever see; and
all he lacked was age to make a name for himself
equal to Captain Kidd or George Washington. I
bet you it would 'a' crowded either of *them* to find
that hill, with all their gifts, but it warn't nothing
to Tom Sawyer; he went across Sahara and put his
finger on it as easy as you could pick a nigger out of
a bunch of angels.

We found a pond of salt - water close by and
scraped up a raft of salt around the edges, and
loaded up the lion's skin and the tiger's so as they
would keep till Jim could tan them.

CHAPTER XI

THE SAND-STORM

WE went a-fooling along for a day or two, and
then just as the full moon was touching the
ground on the other side of the desert, we see a
string of little black figgers moving across its big
silver face. You could see them as plain as if they
was painted on the moon with ink. It was another
caravan. We cooled down our speed and tagged
along after it, just to have company, though it
wain't going our way. It was a rattler, that caravan, and a most bully sight to look at next morning when the sun come a-streaming across the desert and flung the long shadders of the camels on the
gold sand like a thousand grand-daddy-long-legses
marching in procession. We never went very near
it, because we knowed better now than to act like
that and scare people's camels and break up their
caravans. It was the gayest outfit you ever see,
for rich clothes and nobby style. Some of the chiefs
rode on dromedaries, the first we ever see, and very
tall, and they go plunging along like they was on
stilts, and they rock the man that is on them pretty
violent and churn up his dinner considerable, I bet
you, but they make noble good time, and a camel
ain't nowheres with them for speed.

The caravan camped, during the middle part of the day, and then started again about the middle of the afternoon. Before long the sun begun to look very curious. First it kind of turned to brass, and then to copper, and after that it begun to look like a blood-red ball, and the air got hot and close, and pretty soon all the sky in the west darkened up and looked thick and foggy, but fiery and dreadful—like it looks through a piece of red glass, you know. We looked down and see a big confusion going on in the caravan, and a rushing every which way like they was scared; and then they all flopped down flat in the sand and laid there perfectly still.

Pretty soon we see something coming that stood up like an amazing wide wall, and reached from the desert up into the sky and hid the sun, and it was coming like the nation, too. Then a little faint breeze struck us, and then it come harder, and grains of sand begun to sift against our faces and sting like fire, and Tom sung out:

"It's a sand-storm—turn your backs to it!"

We done it; and in another minute it was blowing a gale, and the sand beat against us by the shovelful, and the air was so thick with it we couldn't see a thing. In five minutes the boat was level full, and we was setting on the lockers buried up to the chin in sand, and only our heads out and could hardly breathe.

Then the storm thinned, and we see that monstrous wall go a-sailing off across the desert, awful to look at, I tell you. We dug ourselves out and looked down, and where the caravan was before there wasn't anything but just the sand ocean now, and all still and quiet. All them people and camels was smothered and dead and buried—buried under ten foot of sand, we reckoned, and Tom allowed it might be years before the wind uncovered them, and all that time their friends wouldn't ever know what become of that caravan. Tom said:

"*Now* we know what it was that happened to the people we got the swords and pistols from."

Yes, sir, that was just it. It was as plain as day now. They got buried in a sand-storm, and the wild animals couldn't get at them, and the wind never uncovered them again until they was dried to leather and warn't fit to eat. It seemed to me we had felt as sorry for them poor people as a person could for anybody, and as mournful, too, but we was mistaken; this last caravan's death went harder with us, a good deal harder. You see, the others was total strangers, and we never got to feeling acquainted with them at all, except, maybe, a little with the man that was watching the girl, but it was different with this last caravan. We was huvvering around them a whole night and 'most a whole day, and had got to feeling real friendly with them, and acquainted. I have found out that there ain't no surer way to find out whether you like people or hate them than to travel with them. Just so with these. We kind of liked them from the start, and traveling with them put on the finisher. The longer we traveled with them, and the more we got used to their ways, the better and better we liked them, and the gladder and gladder we was that we run across them. We had come to know some of them so well that we called them by name when we was talking about them, and soon got so familiar and sociable that we even dropped the Miss and Mister and just used their plain names without any handle, and it did not seem unpolite, but just the right thing. Of course, it wasn't their own names, but names we give them. There was Mr. Elexander Robinson and Miss Adaline Robinson, and Colonel Jacob McDougal and Miss Harryet McDougal, and Judge Jeremiah Butler and young Bushrod Butler, and these was big chiefs mostly that wore splendid great turbans and simmeters, and dressed like the Grand Mogul, and their families. But as soon as we come to know them good, and like them very much, it warn't Mister, nor Judge, nor nothing, any more, but only Elleck, and Addy, and Jake, and Hattie, and Jerry, and Buck, and so on.

And you know the more you join in with people in their joys and their sorrows, the more nearer and dearer they come to be to you. Now we warn't cold and indifferent, the way most travelers is, we was right down friendly and sociable, and took a chance in everything that was going, and the caravan could depend on us to be on hand every time, it didn't make no difference what it was.

When they camped, we camped right over them, ten or twelve hundred feet up in the air. When they et a meal, we et ourn, and it made it ever so much homeliker to have their company. When they had a wedding that night, and Buck and Addy got married, we got ourselves up in the very starchiest of the professor's duds for the blow-out, and when they danced we jined in and shook a foot up there.

But it is sorrow and trouble that brings you the nearest, and it was a funeral that done it with us. It was next morning, just in the still dawn. We didn't know the diseased, and he warn't in our set, but that never made no difference; he belonged to the caravan, and that was enough, and there warn't no more sincerer tears shed over him than the ones we dripped on him from up there eleven hundred foot on high.

- Yes, parting with this caravan was much more bitterer than it was to part with them others, which was comparative strangers, and been dead so long, anyway. We had knowed these in their lives, and was fond of them, too, and now to have death snatch them from right before our faces while we was looking, and leave us so lonesome and friendless in the middle of that big desert, it did hurt so, and we wished we mightn't ever make any more friends on that voyage if we was going to lose them again like that.

We couldn't keep from talking about them, and they was all the time coming up in our memory, and looking just the way they looked when we was all alive and happy together. We could see the line marching, and the shiny spearheads a-winking in the sun; we could see the dromedaries lumbering along; we could see the wedding and the funeral; and more oftener than anything else we could see them praying, because they don't allow nothing to prevent that; whenever the call come, several times a day, they would stop right there, and stand up and face to the east, and lift back their heads, and spread out their arms and begin, and four or five times they would go down on their knees, and then fall forward and touch their forehead to the ground.

Well, it warn't good to go on talking about them, lovely as they was in their life, and dear to us in their life and death both, because it didn't do no good, and made us too downhearted. Jim allowed he was going to live as good a life as he could, so he could see them again in a better world; and Tom kept still and didn't tell him they was only Mohammedans; it warn't no use to disappoint him, he was feeling bad enough just as it was.

When we woke up next morning we was feeling a little cheerfuler, and had had a most powerful good sleep, because sand is the comfortablest bed there is, and I don't see why people that can afford it don't have it more. And it's terrible good ballast, too; I never see the balloon so steady before.

Tom allowed we had twenty tons of it, and wondered what we better do with it; it was good sand, and it didn't seem good sense to throw it away. Jim says:

"Mars Tom, can't we tote it back home en sell it? How long 'll it take?"

"Depends on the way we go."

"Well, sah, she's wuth a quarter of a dollar a load at home, en I reckon we's got as much as twenty loads, hain't we? How much would dat be?"

"Five dollars."

"By jings, Mars Tom, le's shove for home right

on de spot! Hit's more'n a dollar en a half apiece, hain't it?"

"Yes."

"Well, ef dat ain't makin' money de easiest ever *I* struck! She jes' rained in—never cos' us a lick o' work. Le's mosey right along, Mars Tom."

But Tom was thinking and ciphering away so busy and excited he never heard him. Pretty soon he says:

"Five dollars—sho! Look here, this sand's worth—worth—why, it's worth no end of money."

"How is dat, Mars Tom? Go on, honey, go on!"

"Well, the minute people knows it's genuwyne sand from the genuwyne Desert of Sahara, they'll just be in a perfect state of mind to git hold of some of it to keep on the what-not in a vial with a label on it for a curiosity. All we got to do is to put it up in vials and float around all over the United States and peddle them out at ten cents apiece. We've got all of ten thousand dollars' worth of sand in this boat."

Me and Jim went all to pieces with joy, and begun to shout whoopjamboreehoo, and Tom says:

"And we can keep on coming back and fetching sand, and coming back and fetching more sand, and just keep it a-going till we've carted this whole desert over there and sold it out; and there ain't ever going to be any opposition, either, because we'll take out a patent."

"My goodness," I says, "we'll be as rich as Creosote, won't we, Tom?"

"Yes—Creesus, you mean. Why, that dervish

was hunting in that little hill for the treasures of the earth, and didn't know he was walking over the real ones for a thousand miles. He was blinder than he made the driver."

"Mars Tom, how much is we gwyne to be worth?"

"Well, I don't know yet. It's got to be ciphered, and it ain't the easiest job to do, either, because it's over four million square miles of sand at ten cents a vial."

Jim was awful excited, but this faded it out considerable, and he shook his head and says:

"Mars Tom, we can't 'ford all dem vials—a king couldn't. We better not try to take de whole desert, Mars Tom, de vials gwyne to bust us, sho'."

Tom's excitement died out, too, now, and I reckoned it was on account of the vials, but it wasn't. He set there thinking, and got bluer and bluer, and at last he says:

"Boys, it won't work; we got to give it up."

"Why, Tom?"

"On account of the duties."

I couldn't make nothing out of that, neither could Jim. I says:

"What *is* our duty, Tom? Because if we can't git around it, why can't we just *do* it? People often has to."

But he says:

"Oh, it ain't that kind of duty. The kind I mean is a tax. Whenever you strike a frontier— that's the border of a country, you know—you find a custom-house there, and the gov'ment officers comes and rummages among your things and charges a big tax, which they call a duty because it's their duty to bust you if they can, and if you don't pay the duty they'll hog your sand. They call it confiscating, but that don't deceive nobody, it's just hogging, and that's all it is. Now if we try to carry this sand home the way we're pointed now, we got to climb fences till we git tired—just frontier after frontier—Egypt, Arabia, Hindustan, and so on, and they'll all whack on a duty, and so you see, easy enough, we *can't* go *that* road."

"Why, Tom," I says, "we can sail right over their old frontiers; how are *they* going to stop us?"

He looked sorrowful at me, and says, very grave:

"Huck Finn, do you think that would be honest?"

I hate them kind of interruptions. I never said nothing, and he went on:

"Well, we're shut off the other way, too. If we go back the way we've come, there's the New York custom-house, and that is worse than all of them others put together, on account of the kind of cargo we've got."

"Why?"

"Well, they can't raise Sahara sand in America, of course, and when they can't raise a thing there, the duty is fourteen hundred thousand per cent. on it if you try to fetch it in from where they do raise it."

"There ain't no sense in that, Tom Sawyer."

"Who said there *was?* What do you talk to me like that for, Huck Finn? You wait till I say a thing's got sense in it before you go to accusing me of saying it."

"All right, consider me crying about it, and sorry. Go on."

Jim says:

"Mars Tom, do dey jam dat duty onto everything we can't raise in America, en don't make no 'stinction 'twix' anything?"

"Yes, that's what they do."

"Mars Tom, ain't de blessin' o' de Lord de mos' valuable thing dey is?"

"Yes, it is."

"Don't de preacher stan' up in de pulpit en call it down on de people?"

"Yes."

"Whah do it come from?"

"From heaven."

"Yassir! you's jes' right, 'deed you is, honey—it come from heaven, en dat's a foreign country. *Now*, den! do dey put a tax on dat blessin'?"

"No, they don't."

"'Course dey don't; en so it stan' to reason dat you's mistaken, Mars Tom. Dey wouldn't put de tax on po' truck like san', dat everybody ain't 'bleeged to have, en leave it off'n de bes' thing dey is, which nobody can't git along widout."

Tom Sawyer was stumped; he see Jim had got him where he couldn't budge. He tried to wiggle out by saying they had *forgot* to put on that tax, but they'd be sure to remember about it, next session of Congress, and then they'd put it on, but that was a poor lame come-off, and he knowed it. He said there warn't nothing foreign that warn't taxed but just that one, and so they couldn't be consistent

without taxing it, and to be consistent was the first
law of politics. So he stuck to it that they'd left it
out unintentional and would be certain to do their
best to fix it before they got caught and laughed at.

But I didn't feel no more interest in such things,
as long as we couldn't git our sand through, and it
made me low-spirited, and Jim the same. Tom he
tried to cheer us up by saying he would think up
another speculation for us that would be just as good
as this one and better, but it didn't do no good, we
didn't believe there was any as big as this. It was
mighty hard; such a little while ago we was so rich,
and could 'a' bought a country and started a kingdom and been celebrated and happy, and now we
was so poor and ornery again, and had our sand left
on our hands. The sand was looking so lovely before, just like gold and di'monds, and the feel of it
was so soft and so silky and nice, but now I couldn't
bear the sight of it, it made me sick to look at it, and
I knowed I wouldn't ever feel comfortable again till
we got shut of it, and I didn't have it there no more
to remind us of what we had been and what we had
got degraded down to. The others was feeling the
same way about it that I was. I knowed it, because
they cheered up so, the minute I says le's throw this
truck overboard.

Well, it was going to be work, you know, and
pretty solid work, too; so Tom he divided it up according to fairness and strength. He said me and
him would clear out a fifth apiece of the sand, and
Jim three-fifths. Jim he didn't quite like that arrangement. He says:

"'Course I's de stronges', en I's willin' to do a share accordin', but by jings you's kinder pilin' it onto ole Jim, Mars Tom, hain't you?"

"Well, I didn't think so, Jim, but you try your hand at fixing it, and let's see."

So Jim reckoned it wouldn't be no more than fair if me and Tom done a *tenth* apiece. Tom he turned his back to git room and be private, and then he smole a smile that spread around and covered the whole Sahara to the westward, back to the Atlantic edge of it where we come from. Then he turned around again and said it was a good enough arrangement, and we was satisfied if Jim was. Jim said he was.

So then Tom measured off our two-tenths in the bow and left the rest for Jim, and it surprised Jim a good deal to see how much difference there was and what a raging lot of sand his share come to, and said he was powerful glad now that he had spoke up in time and got the first arrangement altered, for he said that even the way it was now, there was more sand than enjoyment in his end of the con-tract, he believed.

Then we laid into it. It was mighty hot work, and tough; so hot we had to move up into cooler weather or we couldn't 'a' stood it. Me and Tom took turn about, and one worked while t'other rested, but there warn't nobody to spell poor old Jim, and he made all that part of Africa damp, he sweated so. We couldn't work good, we was so full of laugh, and Jim he kept fretting and wanting to know what tickled us so, and we had to keep making up things to account for it, and they was pretty poor inventions, but they done well enough, Jim didn't see through them. At last when we got done we was 'most dead, but not with work but with laughing. By and by Jim was 'most dead, too, but it was with work; then we took turns and spelled him, and he was as thankful as he could be, and would set on the gunnel and swab the sweat, and heave and pant, and say how good we was to a poor old nigger, and he wouldn't ever forgit us. He was always the gratefulest nigger I ever see, for any little thing you done for him. He was only nigger outside; inside he was as white as you be.

CHAPTER XII

JIM STANDING SIEGE

THE next few meals was pretty sandy, but that don't make no difference when you are hungry; and when you ain't it ain't no satisfaction to eat, anyway, and so a little grit in the meat ain't no particular drawback, as far as I can see.

Then we struck the east end of the desert at last, sailing on a northeast course. Away off on the edge of the sand, in a soft pinky light, we see three little sharp roofs like tents, and Tom says:

"It's the pyramids of Egypt."

It made my heart fairly jump. You see, I had seen a many and a many a picture of them, and heard tell about them a hundred times, and yet to come on them all of a sudden, that way, and find they was *real*, 'stead of imaginations, 'most knocked the breath out of me with surprise. It's a curious thing, that the more you hear about a grand and big and bully thing or person, the more it kind of dreamies out, as you may say, and gets to be a big dim wavery figger made out of moonshine and nothing solid to it. It's just so with George Washington, and the same with them pyramids.

And moreover, besides the thing they always said about them seemed to me to be stretchers. There was a feller come to the Sunday-school once, and had a picture of them, and made a speech, and said the biggest pyramid covered thirteen acres, and was most five hundred foot high, just a steep mountain, all built out of hunks of stone as big as a bureau, and laid up in perfectly regular layers, like stair-steps. Thirteen acres, you see, for just one building; it's a farm. If it hadn't been in Sunday-school, I would 'a' judged it was a lie; and outside I was certain of it. And he said there was a hole in the pyramid, and you could go in there with candles, and go ever so far up a long slanting tunnel, and come to a large room in the stomach of that stone mountain, and there you would find a big stone chest with a king in it, four thousand years old. I said to myself, then, if that ain't a lie I will eat that king if they will fetch him, for even Methusalem warn't that old, and nobody claims it.

As we come a little nearer we see the yaller sand come to an end in a long straight edge like a blanket, and onto it was joined, edge to edge, a wide country of bright green, with a snaky stripe crooking through it, and Tom said it was the Nile. It made my heart jump again, for the Nile was another thing that wasn't real to me. Now I can tell you one thing which is dead certain: if you will fool along over three thousand miles of yaller sand, all glimmering with heat so that it makes your eyes water to look at it, and you've been a considerable part of a week doing it, the green country will look so like home and heaven to you that it will make your eyes water *again*.

It was just so with me, and the same with Jim.

And when Jim got so he could believe it *was* the land of Egypt he was looking at, he wouldn't enter it standing up, but got down on his knees and took off his hat, because he said it wasn't fitten' for a humble poor nigger to come any other way where such men had been as Moses and Joseph and Pharaoh and the other prophets. He was a Presbyterian, and had a most deep respect for Moses, which was a Presbyterian, too, he said. He was all stirred up, and says:

"Hit's de lan' of Egypt, de lan' of Egypt, en I's 'lowed to look at it wid my own eyes! En dah's de river dat was turn' to blood, en I's looking at de very same groun' whah de plagues was, en de lice, en de frogs, en de locus', en de hail, en whah dey marked de door-pos', en de angel o' de Lord come by in de darkness o' de night en slew de fust-born in all de lan' o' Egypt. Ole Jim ain't worthy to see dis day!"

And then he just broke down and cried, he was so thankful. So between him and Tom there was talk enough, Jim being excited because the land was so full of history—Joseph and his brethren, Moses in the bulrushers, Jacob coming down into Egypt to buy corn, the silver cup in the sack, and all them interesting things; and Tom just as excited too, because the land was so full of history that was in *his* line, about Noureddin, and Bedreddin, and such like monstrous giants, that made Jim's wool rise, and a raft of other *Arabian Nights* folks, which the half of them never done the things they let on they done, I don't believe.

Then we struck a disappointment, for one of them early morning fogs started up, and it warn't no use to sail over the top of it, because we would go by Egypt, sure, so we judged it was best to set her by compass straight for the place where the pyramids was gitting blurred and blotted out, and then drop low and skin along pretty close to the ground and keep a sharp lookout. Tom took the hellum, I stood by to let go the anchor, and Jim he straddled the bow to dig through the fog with his eyes and watch out for danger ahead. We went along a steady gait, but not very fast, and the fog got solider and solider, so solid that Jim looked dim and ragged and smoky through it. It was awful still, and we talked low and was anxious. Now and then Jim would say:

"Highst her a p'int, Mars Tom, highst her!" and up she would skip, a foot or two, and we would slide right over a flat-roofed mud cabin, with people that had been asleep on it just beginning to turn out and gap and stretch; and once when a feller was clear up on his hind legs so he could gap and stretch better, we took him a blip in the back and knocked him off. By and by, after about an hour, and everything dead still and we a-straining our ears for sounds and holding our breath, the fog thinned a little, very sudden, and Jim sung out in an awful scare:

"Oh, for de lan's sake, set her back, Mars Tom, here's de biggest giant outen de *'Rabian Nights* a-comin' for us!" and he went over backwards in the boat.

Tom slammed on the back-action, and as we

slowed to a standstill a man's face as big as our house at home looked in over the gunnel, same as a house looks out of its windows, and I laid down and died. I must 'a' been clear dead and gone for as much as a minute or more; then I come to, and Tom had hitched a boat-hook onto the lower lip of the giant and was holding the balloon steady with it whilst he canted his head back and got a good long look up at that awful face.

Jim was on his knees with his hands clasped, gazing up at the thing in a begging way, and working his lips, but not getting anything out. I took only just a glimpse, and was fading out again, but Tom says:

"He ain't alive, you fools; it's the Sphinx!"

I never see Tom look so little and like a fly; but that was because the giant's head was so big and awful. Awful, yes, so it was, but not dreadful any more, because you could see it was a noble face, and kind of sad, and not thinking about you, but about other things and larger. It was stone, reddish stone, and its nose and ears battered, and that give it an abused look, and you felt sorrier for it for that.

We stood off a piece, and sailed around it and over it, and it was just grand. It was a man's head, or maybe a woman's, on a tiger's body a hundred and twenty-five foot long, and there was a dear little temple between its front paws. All but the head used to be under the sand, for hundreds of years, maybe thousands, but they had just lately dug the sand away and found that little temple. It took a power of sand to bury that cretur; most as much as it would to bury a steamboat, I reckon.

We landed Jim on top of the head, with an American flag to protect him, it being a foreign land; then we sailed off to this and that and t'other distance, to git what Tom called effects and perspectives and proportions, and Jim he done the best he could, striking all the different kinds of attitudes and positions he could study up, but standing on his head and working his legs the way a frog does was the best. The further we got away, the littler Jim got, and the grander the Sphinx got, till at last it was only a clothes-pin on a dome, as you might say. That's the way perspective brings out the correct proportions, Tom said; he said Julus Cesar's niggers didn't know how big he was, they was too close to him.

Then we sailed off further and further, till we couldn't see Jim at all any more, and then that great figger was at its noblest, a-gazing out over the Nile Valley so still and solemn and lonesome, and all the little shabby huts and things that was scattered about it clean disappeared and gone, and nothing around it now but a soft wide spread of yaller velvet, which was the sand.

That was the right place to stop, and we done it. We set there a-looking and a-thinking for a half an hour, nobody a-saying anything, for it made us feel quiet and kind of solemn to remember it had been looking over that valley just that same way, and thinking its awful thoughts all to itself for thousands of years, and nobody can't find out what they are to this day.

At last I took up the glass and see some little black things a-capering around on that velvet carpet, and some more a-climbing up the cretur's back, and then I see two or three wee puffs of white smoke, and told Tom to look. He done it, and says:

"They're bugs. No—hold on; they—why, I believe they're men. Yes, it's men—men and horses both. They're hauling a long ladder up onto the Sphinx's back—now ain't that odd? And now they're trying to lean it up a—there's some more puffs of smoke—it's guns! Huck, they're after Jim."

We clapped on the power, and went for them a-biling. We was there in no time, and come a-whizzing down amongst them, and they broke and scattered every which way, and some that was climbing the ladder after Jim let go all holts and fell. We soared up and found him laying on top of the head panting and most tuckered out, partly from howling for help and partly from scare. He had been standing a siege a long time—a week, *he* said, but it warn't so, it only just seemed so to him because they was crowding him so. They had shot at him, and rained the bullets all around him, but he warn't hit, and when they found he wouldn't stand up and the bullets couldn't git at him when he was laying down, they went for the ladder, and then he knowed it was all up with him if we didn't come pretty quick. Tom was very indignant, and asked him why he didn't show the flag and command them to *git*, in the name of the United States. Jim said he done it, but they never paid no attention. Tom said he would have this thing looked into at Washington, and says:

"You'll see that they'll have to apologize for insulting the flag, and pay an indemnity, too, on top of it, even if they git off *that* easy."

Jim says:

"What's an indemnity, Mars Tom?"

"It's cash, that's what it is."

"Who gits it, Mars Tom?"

"Why, *we* do."

"En who gits de apology?"

"The United States. Or, we can take whichever we please. We can take the apology, if we want to, and let the gov'ment take the money."

"How much money will it be, Mars Tom?"

"Well, in an aggravated case like this one, it will be at least three dollars apiece, and I don't know but more."

"Well, den, we'll take de money, Mars Tom, blame de 'pology. Hain't dat yo' notion, too? En hain't it yourn, Huck?"

We talked it over a little and allowed that that was as good a way as any, so we agreed to take the money. It was a new business to me, and I asked Tom if countries always apologized when they had done wrong, and he says:

"Yes; the little ones does."

We was sailing around examining the pyramids, you know, and now we soared up and roosted on the flat top of the biggest one, and found it was just like what the man said in the Sunday-school. It was like four pairs of stairs that start broad at the bottom and slants up and comes together in a point at the top, only these stair-steps couldn't be clumb the way you climb other stairs; no, for each step was as high as your chin, and you have to be boosted up from behind. The two other pyramids warn't far away, and the people moving about on the sand between looked like bugs crawling, we was so high above them.

Tom he couldn't hold himself he was so worked up with gladness and astonishment to be in such a celebrated place, and he just dripped history from every pore, seemed to me. He said he couldn't scarcely believe he was standing on the very identical spot the prince flew from on the Bronze Horse. It was in the *Arabian Night* times, he said. Somebody give the prince a bronze horse with a peg in its shoulder, and he could git on him and fly through the air like a bird, and go all over the world, and steer it by turning the peg, and fly high or low and land wherever he wanted to.

When he got done telling it there was one of them uncomfortable silences that comes, you know, when a person has been telling a whopper and you feel sorry for him and wish you could think of some way to change the subject and let him down easy, but git stuck and don't see no way, and before you can pull your mind together and *do* something, that silence has got in and spread itself and done the business. I was embarrassed, Jim he was embarrassed, and neither of us couldn't say a word. Well, Tom he glowered at me a minute, and says:

"Come, out with it. What do you think?"

I says:

"Tom Sawyer, *you* don't believe that, yourself."

"What's the reason I don't? What's to hender me?"

"There's one thing to hender you: it couldn't happen, that's all."

"What's the reason it couldn't happen?"

"You tell me the reason it *could* happen."

"This balloon is a good enough reason it could happen, I should reckon."

"*Why* is it?"

"*Why* is it? I never saw such an idiot. Ain't this balloon and the bronze horse the same thing under different names?"

"No, they're not. One is a balloon and the other's a horse. It's very different. Next you'll be saying a house and a cow is the same thing."

"By Jackson, Huck's got him ag'in! Dey ain't no wigglin' outer dat!"

"Shut your head, Jim; you don't know what you're talking about. And Huck don't. Look here, Huck, I'll make it plain to you, so you can understand. You see, it ain't the mere *form* that's got anything to do with their being similar or unsimilar, it's the *principle* involved; and the principle is the same in both. Don't you see, now?"

I turned it over in my mind, and says:

"Tom, it ain't no use. Principles is all very well, but they don't git around that one big fact, that the thing that a balloon can do ain't no sort of proof of what a horse can do."

"Shucks, Huck, you don't get the idea at all.

Now look here a minute—it's perfectly plain. Don't we fly through the air?"

"Yes."

"Very well. Don't we fly high or fly low, just as we please?"

"Yes."

"Don't we steer whichever way we want to?"

"Yes."

"And don't we land when and where we please?"

"Yes."

"How do we move the balloon and steer it?"

"By touching the buttons."

"*Now* I reckon the thing is clear to you at last. In the other case the moving and steering was done by turning a peg. We touch a button, the prince turned a peg. There ain't an atom of difference, you see. I knowed I could git it through your head if I stuck to it long enough."

He felt so happy he begun to whistle. But me and Jim was silent, so he broke off surprised, and says:

"Looky here, Huck Finn, don't you see it *yet?*"

I says:

"Tom Sawyer, I want to ask you some questions."

"Go ahead," he says, and I see Jim chirk up to listen.

"As I understand it, the whole thing is in the buttons and the peg — the rest ain't of no consequence. A button is one shape, a peg is another shape, but that ain't any matter?"

"No, that ain't any matter, as long as they've both got the same power."

"All right, then. What is the power that's in a candle and in a match?"

"It's the fire."

"It's the same in both, then?"

"Yes, just the same in both."

"All right. Suppose I set fire to a carpenter shop with a match, what will happen to that carpenter shop?"

"She'll burn up."

"And suppose I set fire to this pyramid with a candle—will she burn up?"

"Of course she won't."

"All right. Now the fire's the same, both times. *Why* does the shop burn, and the pyramid don't?"

"Because the pyramid *can't* burn."

"Aha! and *a horse can't fly!*"

"My lan', ef Huck ain't got him ag'in! Huck's landed him high en dry dis time, *I* tell you! Hit's de smartes' trap I ever see a body walk inter—en ef I—"

But Jim was so full of laugh he got to strangling and couldn't go on, and Tom was that mad to see how neat I had floored him, and turned his own argument ag'in him and knocked him all to rags and flinders with it, that all he could manage to say was that whenever he heard me and Jim try to argue it made him ashamed of the human race. I never said nothing; I was feeling pretty well satisfied. When I have got the best of a person that way, it ain't my way to go around crowing about it the way some people does, for I consider that if I was in his place I wouldn't wish him to crow over me. It's better to be generous, that's what I think.

CHAPTER XIII

GOING FOR TOM'S PIPE

BY AND BY we left Jim to float around up there in the neighborhood of the pyramids, and we clumb down to the hole where you go into the tunnel, and went in with some Arabs and candles, and away in there in the middle of the pyramid we found a room and a big stone box in it where they used to keep that king, just as the man in the Sunday-school said; but he was gone, now; somebody had got him. But I didn't take no interest in the place, because there could be ghosts there, of course; not fresh ones, but I don't like no kind.

So then we come out and got some little donkeys and rode a piece, and then went in a boat another piece, and then more donkeys, and got to Cairo; and all the way the road was as smooth and beautiful a road as ever I see, and had tall date-pa'ms on both sides, and naked children everywhere, and the men was as red as copper, and fine and strong and handsome. And the city was a curiosity. Such narrow streets—why, they were just lanes, and crowded with people with turbans, and women with veils, and everybody rigged out in blazing bright clothes and all sorts of colors, and you wondered how the camels and the people got by each other in such narrow little cracks, but they done it—a perfect jam, you see, and everybody noisy. The stores warn't big enough to turn around in, but you didn't have to go in; the storekeeper sat tailor fashion on his counter, smoking his snaky long pipe, and had his things where he could reach them to sell, and he was just as good as in the street, for the camel-loads brushed him as they went by.

Now and then a grand person flew by in a carriage with fancy dressed men running and yelling in front of it and whacking anybody with a long rod that didn't get out of the way. And by and by along comes the Sultan riding horseback at the head of a procession, and fairly took your breath away, his clothes was so splendid; and everybody fell flat and laid on his stomach while he went by. I forgot, but a feller helped me to remember. He was one that had a rod and run in front.

There was churches, but they don't know enough to keep Sunday; they keep Friday and break the Sabbath. You have to take off your shoes when you go in. There was crowds of men and boys in the church, setting in groups on the stone floor and making no end of noise—getting their lessons by heart, Tom said, out of the Koran, which they think is a Bible, and people that knows better knows enough to not let on. I never see such a big church in my life before, and most awful high, it was; it made you dizzy to look up; our village church at home ain't a circumstance to it; if you was to put it in there, people would think it was a dry-goods box.

What I wanted to see was a dervish, because I was interested in dervishes on account of the one that played the trick on the camel-driver. So we found a lot in a kind of a church, and they called themselves Whirling Dervishes; and they did whirl, too. I never see anything like it. They had tall sugar-loaf hats on, and linen petticoats; and they spun and spun and spun, round and round like tops, and the petticoats stood out on a slant, and it was the prettiest thing I ever see, and made me drunk to look at it. They was all Moslems, Tom said, and when I asked him what a Moslem was, he said it was a person that wasn't a Presbyterian. So there is plenty of them in Missouri, though I didn't know it before.

We didn't see half there was to see in Cairo, because Tom was in such a sweat to hunt out places that was celebrated in history. We had a most tiresome time to find the granary where Joseph stored up the grain before the famine, and when we found it it warn't worth much to look at, being such an old tumbledown wreck; but Tom was satisfied, and made more fuss over it than I would make if I stuck a nail in my foot. How he ever found that place was too many for me. We passed as much as forty just like it before we come to it, and any of them would 'a' done for me, but none but just the right one would suit him; I never see anybody so particular as Tom Sawyer. The minute he struck the right one he reconnized it as easy as I would reconnize my other shirt if I had one, but how he done it he couldn't any more tell than he could fly; he said so himself.

Then we hunted a long time for the house where
the boy lived that learned the cadi how to try the
case of the old olives and the new ones, and said it
was out of the *Arabian Nights,* and he would tell me
and Jim about it when he got time.   Well, we hunted
and hunted till I was ready to drop, and I wanted
Tom to give it up and come next day and git somebody that knowed the town and could talk Mis-
sourian and could go straight to the place; but no,
he wanted to find it himself, and nothing else would
answer.   So on we went.   Then at last the remark-
ablest thing happened I ever see.   The house was
gone—gone hundreds of years ago—every last rag
of it gone but just one mud brick.   Now a person
wouldn't ever believe that a backwoods Missouri
boy that hadn't ever been in that town before could
go and hunt that place over and find that brick, but
Tom Sawyer done it.   I know he done it, because I
see him do it.   I was right by his very side at the
time, and see him see the brick and see him reconnize
it.   Well, I says to myself, how *does* he do it?   Is it
knowledge, or is it instink?

Now there's the facts, just as they happened: let
everybody explain it their own way.   I've ciphered
over it a good deal, and it's my opinion that some of
it is knowledge but the main bulk of it is instink.
The reason is this: Tom put the brick in his pocket
to give to a museum with his name on it and the
facts when he went home, and I slipped it out and
put another brick considerable like it in its place,
and he didn't know the difference—but there was
a difference, you see.   I think that settles it—it's

mostly instink, not knowledge. Instink tells him
where the exact *place* is for the brick to be in, and
so he reconnizes it by the place it's in, not by the
look of the brick. If it was knowledge, not instink,
he would know the brick again by the look of it the
next time he seen it—which he didn't. So it shows
that for all the brag you hear about knowledge being
such a wonderful thing, instink is worth forty of it
for real unerringness. Jim says the same.

When we got back Jim dropped down and took us
in, and there was a young man there with a red
skull-cap and tassel on and a beautiful silk jacket
and baggy trousers with a shawl around his waist
and pistols in it that could talk English and wanted
to hire to us as guide and take us to Mecca and
Medina and Central Africa and everywheres for a
half a dollar a day and his keep, and we hired him and
left, and piled on the power, and by the time we was
through dinner we was over the place where the
Israelites crossed the Red Sea when Pharaoh tried
to overtake them and was caught by the waters.
We stopped, then, and had a good look at the place,
and it done Jim good to see it. He said he could see
it all, now, just the way it happened; he could see the
Israelites walking along between the walls of water,
and the Egyptians coming, from away off yonder,
hurrying all they could, and see them start in as the
Israelites went out, and then when they was all in,
see the walls tumble together and drown the last
man of them. Then we piled on the power again
and rushed away and huvvered over Mount Sinai,
and saw the place where Moses broke the tables

of stone, and where the children of Israel camped in the plain and worshiped the golden calf, and it was all just as interesting as could be, and the guide knowed every place as well as I knowed the village at home.

But we had an accident, now, and it fetched all the plans to a standstill. Tom's old ornery corn-cob pipe had got so old and swelled and warped that she couldn't hold together any longer, notwith-standing the strings and bandages, but caved in and went to pieces. Tom he didn't know *what* to do. The professor's pipe wouldn't answer; it warn't any-thing but a mershum, and a person that's got used to a cob pipe knows it lays a long ways over all the other pipes in this world, and you can't git him to smoke any other. He wouldn't take mine, I couldn't persuade him. So there he was.

He thought it over, and said we must scour around and see if we could roust out one in Egypt or Arabia or around in some of these countries, but the guide said no, it warn't no use, they didn't have them. So Tom was pretty glum for a little while, then he chirked up and said he'd got the idea and knowed what to do. He says:

"I've got another corn-cob pipe, and it's a prime one, too, and nearly new. It's laying on the rafter that's right over the kitchen stove at home in the village. Jim, you and the guide will go and get it, and me and Huck will camp here on Mount Sinai till you come back."

"But, Mars Tom, we couldn't ever find de village. I could find de pipe, 'case I knows de kitchen, but, my lan', *we* can't ever find de village, nur Sent Louis, nur none o' dem places. We don't know de way, Mars Tom."

That was a fact, and it stumped Tom for a minute. Then he said:

"Looky here, it can be done, sure; and I'll tell you how. You set your compass and sail west as straight as a dart, till you find the United States. It ain't any trouble, because it's the first land you'll strike the other side of the Atlantic. If it's daytime when you strike it, bulge right on, straight west from the upper part of the Florida coast, and in an hour and three-quarters you'll hit the mouth of the Mississippi—at the speed that I'm going to send you. You'll be so high up in the air that the earth will be curved considerable—sorter like a washbowl turned upside down—and you'll see a raft of rivers crawling around every which way, long before you get there, and you can pick out the Mississippi without any trouble. Then you can follow the river north nearly, an hour and three-quarters, till you see the Ohio come in; then you want to look sharp, because you're getting near. Away up to your left you'll see another thread coming in — that's the Missouri and is a little above St. Louis. You'll come down low then, so as you can examine the villages as you spin along. You'll pass about twenty-five in the next fifteen minutes, and you'll recognize ours when you see it—and if you don't you can yell down and ask."

"Ef it's dat easy, Mars Tom, I reckon we kin do it—yassir, I knows we kin."

The guide was sure of it, too, and thought that he could learn to stand his watch in a little while.

"Jim can learn you the whole thing in a half an hour," Tom said. "This balloon's as easy to manage as a canoe."

Tom got out the chart and marked out the course and measured it, and says:

"To go back west is the shortest way, you see. It's only about seven thousand miles. If you went east, and so on around, it's over twice as far." Then he says to the guide, "I want you both to watch the telltale all through the watches, and whenever it don't mark three hundred miles an hour, you go higher or drop lower till you find a storm-current that's going your way. There's a hundred miles an hour in this old thing without any wind to help. There's two-hundred-mile gales to be found, any time you want to hunt for them."

"We'll hunt for them, sir."

"See that you do. Sometimes you may have to go up a couple of miles, and it 'll be p'ison cold, but most of the time you'll find your storm a good deal lower. If you can only strike a cyclone—that's the ticket for you! You'll see by the professor's books that they travel west in these latitudes; and they travel low, too."

Then he ciphered on the time, and says:

"Seven thousand miles, three hundred miles an hour—you can make the trip in a day—twenty-four hours. This is Thursday; you'll be back here Saturday afternoon. Come, now, hustle out some blankets and food and books and things for me and Huck. and you can start right along. There ain't no

MAP
OF
THE TRIP
made by
Tom Sawyer
Erro no te go

occasion to fool around—I want a smoke, and the quicker you fetch that pipe the better.''

All hands jumped for the things, and in eight minutes our things was out and the balloon was ready for America. So we shook hands good-by, and Tom gave his last orders:

"It's ten minutes to 2 P.M. now, Mount Sinai time. In twenty-four hours you'll be home, and it 'll be six to-morrow morning, village time. When you strike the village, land a little back of the top of the hill, in the woods, out of sight; then you rush down, Jim, and shove these letters in the post-office, and if you see anybody stirring, pull your slouch down over your face so they won't know you. Then you go and slip in the back way to the kitchen and git the pipe, and lay this piece of paper on the kitchen table, and put something on it to hold it, and then slide out and git away, and don't let Aunt Polly catch a sight of you, nor nobody else. Then you jump for the balloon and shove for Mount Sinai three hundred miles an hour. You won't have lost more than an hour. You'll start back at 7 or 8 A.M., village time, and be here in twenty-four hours, arriving at 2 or 3 P.M., Mount Sinai time.''

Tom he read the piece of paper to us. He had wrote on it:

"THURSDAY AFTERNOON. *Tom Sawyer the Erronort sends his love to Aunt Polly from Mount Sinai where the Ark was,*[1] *and so does Huck Finn, and she will get it to-morrow morning half-past six.*

"TOM SAWYER THE ERRONORT.''

[1] This misplacing of the Ark is probably Huck's error, not Tom's. —M. T.

"That 'll make her eyes bulge out and the tears come," he says. Then he says:

"Stand by! One—two—three—away you go!"

And away she *did* go! Why, she seemed to whiz out of sight in a second.

Then we found a most comfortable cave that looked out over the whole big plain, and there we camped to wait for the pipe.

The balloon come back all right, and brung the pipe; but Aunt Polly had catched Jim when he was getting it, and anybody can guess what happened: she sent for Tom. So Jim he says:

"Mars Tom, she's out on de porch wid her eye sot on de sky a-layin' for you, en she say she ain't gwyne to budge from dah tell she gits hold of you. Dey's gwyne to be trouble, Mars Tom, 'deed dey is."

So then we shoved for home, and not feeling very gay, neither.

THE GREAT REVOLUTION
IN PITCAIRN

LET me refresh the reader's memory a little.
Nearly a hundred years ago the crew of the
British ship *Bounty* mutinied, set the captain and
his officers adrift upon the open sea, took possession
of the ship, and sailed southward. They procured
wives for themselves among the natives of Tahiti,
then proceeded to a lonely little rock in mid-Pacific,
called Pitcairn's Island, wrecked the vessel, stripped
her of everything that might be useful to a new
colony, and established themselves on shore.

Pitcairn's is so far removed from the track of com-
merce that it was many years before another vessel
touched there. It had always been considered an
uninhabited island; so when a ship did at last drop
its anchor there, in 1808, the captain was greatly
surprised to find the place peopled. Although the
mutineers had fought among themselves, and gradu-
ally killed each other off until only two or three of
the original stock remained, these tragedies had not
occurred before a number of children had been born;
so in 1808 the island had a population of twenty-
seven persons. John Adams, the chief mutineer, still
survived, and was to live many years yet, as governor
and patriarch of the flock. From being mutineer

and homicide, he had turned Christian and teacher, and his nation of twenty-seven persons was now the purest and devoutest in Christendom. Adams had long ago hoisted the British flag and constituted his island an appanage of the British crown.

To-day the population numbers ninety persons—sixteen men, nineteen women, twenty-five boys, and thirty girls—all descendants of the mutineers, all bearing the family names of those mutineers, and all speaking English, and English only. The island stands high up out of the sea, and has precipitous walls. It is about three-quarters of a mile long, and in places is as much as half a mile wide. Such arable land as it affords is held by the several families, according to a division made many years ago. There is some live stock—goats, pigs, chickens, and cats; but no dogs, and no large animals. There is one church-building—used also as a capitol, a school-house, and a public library. The title of the governor has been, for a generation or two, "Magistrate and Chief Ruler, in subordination to her Majesty the Queen of Great Britain." It was his province to *make* the laws, as well as execute them. His office was elective; everybody over seventeen years old had a vote—no matter about the sex.

The sole occupations of the people were farming and fishing; their sole recreation, religious services. There has never been a shop in the island, nor any money. The habits and dress of the people have always been primitive, and their laws simple to puerility. They have lived in a deep Sabbath tranquillity, far from the world and its ambitions and vexations, and neither knowing nor caring what was going on in the mighty empires that lie beyond their limitless ocean solitudes. Once in three or four years a ship touched there, moved them with aged news of bloody battles, devastating epidemics, fallen thrones, and ruined dynasties, then traded them some soap and flannel for some yams and breadfruit, and sailed away, leaving them to retire into their peaceful dreams and pious dissipations once more.

On the 8th of last September, Admiral de Horsey, commander-in-chief of the British fleet in the Pacific, visited Pitcairn's Island, and speaks as follows in his official report to the admiralty:

They have beans, carrots, turnips, cabbages, and a little maize; pineapples, fig trees, custard-apples, and oranges; lemons, and cocoanuts. Clothing is obtained alone from passing ships, in barter for refreshments. There are no springs on the island, but as it rains generally once a month they have plenty of water, although at times in former years they have suffered from drought. No alcoholic liquors, except for medicinal purposes, are used, and a drunkard is unknown. . . .

The necessary articles required by the islanders are best shown by those we furnished in barter for refreshments: namely, flannel, serge, drill, half-boots, combs, tobacco, and soap. They also stand much in need of maps and slates for their school, and tools of any kind are most acceptable. I caused them to be supplied from the public stores with a Union Jack for display on the arrival of ships, and a pit-saw, of which they were greatly in need. This, I trust, will meet the approval of their lordships. If the munificent people of England were only aware of the wants of this most deserving little colony, they would not long go unsupplied. . . .

Divine service is held every Sunday at 10.30 A.M. and at 3 P.M., in the house built and used by John Adams for that purpose until he died in 1829. It is conducted strictly in accordance with the liturgy of the Church of England, by Mr. Simon

Young, their selected pastor, who is much respected. A Bible class is held every Wednesday, when all who conveniently can attend. There is also a general meeting for prayer on the first Friday in every month. Family prayers are said in every house the first thing in the morning and the last thing in the evening, and no food is partaken of without asking God's blessing before and afterward. Of these islanders' religious attributes no one can speak without deep respect. A people whose greatest pleasure and privilege is to commune in prayer with their God, and to join in hymns of praise, and who are, moreover, cheerful, diligent, and probably freer from vice than any other community, need no priest among them.

Now I come to a sentence in the admiral's report which he dropped carelessly from his pen, no doubt, and never gave the matter a second thought. He little imagined what a freight of tragic prophecy it bore! This is the sentence:

One stranger, an American, has settled on the island—*a doubtful acquisition.*

A doubtful acquisition, indeed! Captain Ormsby, in the American ship *Hornet*, touched at Pitcairn's nearly four months after the admiral's visit, and from the facts which he gathered there we now know all about that American. Let us put these facts together in historical form. The American's name was Butterworth Stavely. As soon as he had become well acquainted with all the people—and this took but a few days, of course—he began to ingratiate himself with them by all the arts he could command. He became exceedingly popular, and much looked up to; for one of the first things he did was to forsake his worldly way of life, and throw all his energies into religion. He was always reading his Bible, or praying, or singing hymns, or asking blessings. In prayer, no one had such "liberty" as he, no one could pray so long or so well.

At last, when he considered the time to be ripe, he began secretly to sow the seeds of discontent among the people. It was his deliberate purpose, from the beginning, to subvert the government, but of course he kept that to himself for a time. He used different arts with different individuals. He awakened dissatisfaction in one quarter by calling attention to the shortness of the Sunday services; he argued that there should be three three-hour services on Sunday instead of only two. Many had secretly held this opinion before; they now privately banded themselves into a party to work for it. He showed certain of the women that they were not allowed sufficient voice in the prayer-meetings; thus another party was formed. No weapon was beneath his notice; he even descended to the children, and awoke discontent in their breasts because—as *he* discovered for them—they had not enough Sunday-school. This created a third party.

Now, as the chief of these parties, he found himself the strongest power in the community. So he proceeded to his next move—a no less important one than the impeachment of the chief magistrate, James Russell Nickoy; a man of character and ability, and possessed of great wealth, he being the owner of a house with a parlor to it, three acres and a half of yam-land, and the only boat in Pitcairn's, a whale-boat; and, most unfortunately, a pretext for this impeachment offered itself at just the right time.

One of the earliest and most precious laws of the island was the law against trespass. It was held in great reverence, and was regarded as the palladium of the people's liberties. About thirty years ago an important case came before the courts under this law, in this wise: a chicken belonging to Elizabeth Young (aged, at that time, fifty-eight, a daughter of John Mills, one of the mutineers of the *Bounty*) trespassed upon the grounds of Thursday October Christian (aged twenty-nine, a grandson of Fletcher Christian, one of the mutineers). Christian killed the chicken. According to the law, Christian could keep the chicken; or, if he preferred, he could restore its remains to the owner and receive damages in "produce" to an amount equivalent to the waste and injury wrought by the trespasser. The court records set forth that "the said Christian aforesaid did deliver the aforesaid remains to the said Elizabeth Young, and did demand one bushel of yams in satisfaction of the damage done." But Elizabeth Young considered the demand exorbitant; the parties could not agree; therefore Christian brought suit in the courts. He lost his case in the justice's court; at least, he was awarded only a half-peck of yams, which he considered insufficient, and in the nature of a defeat. He appealed. The case lingered several years in an ascending grade of courts, and always resulted in decrees sustaining the original verdict; and finally the thing got into the supreme court, and there it stuck for twenty years. But last summer, even the supreme court managed to arrive at a decision at last. Once more the original verdict was sustained. Christian then said he was satisfied; but Stavely was present, and whispered to him and to his lawyer, suggesting, "as a mere form," that the original law be exhibited, in order to make sure that it still existed. It seemed an odd idea, but an ingenious one. So the demand was made. A messenger was sent to the magistrate's house; he presently returned with the tidings that it had disappeared from among the state archives.

The court now pronounced its late decision void, since it had been made under a law which had no actual existence.

Great excitement ensued immediately. The news swept abroad over the whole island that the palladium of the public liberties was lost—maybe treasonably destroyed. Within thirty minutes almost the entire nation were in the court-room—that is to say, the church. The impeachment of the chief magistrate followed, upon Stavely's motion. The accused met his misfortune with the dignity which became his great office. He did not plead, or even argue; he offered the simple defense that he had not meddled with the missing law; that he had kept the state archives in the same candle-box that had been used as their depository from the beginning; and that he was innocent of the removal or destruction of the lost document.

But nothing could save him; he was found guilty of misprision of treason, and degraded from his office, and all his property was confiscated.

The lamest part of the whole shameful matter was the *reason* suggested by his enemies for his destruction of the law, to wit: that he did it to favor Christian, because Christian was his cousin! Whereas Stavely was the only individual in the entire nation who was *not* his cousin. The reader must remember that all these people are the descendants of half a dozen men; that the first children intermarried together and bore grandchildren to the mutineers; that these grandchildren intermarried; after them, great and great-great-grandchildren intermarried; so that to-day everybody is blood kin to everybody. Moreover, the relationships are wonderfully, even astoundingly, mixed up and complicated. A stranger, for instance, says to an islander:

"You speak of that young woman as your cousin; a while ago you called her your aunt."

"Well, she *is* my aunt, and my cousin, too. And also my stepsister, my niece, my fourth cousin, my thirty-third cousin, my forty-second cousin, my greataunt, my grandmother, my widowed sister-in-law—and next week she will be my wife."

So the charge of nepotism against the chief magistrate was weak. But no matter; weak or strong, it suited Stavely. Stavely was immediately elected to the vacant magistracy, and, oozing reform from every pore, he went vigorously to work. In no long time religious services raged everywhere and unceasingly. By command, the second prayer of the Sunday morning service, which had customarily endured some thirty-five or forty minutes, and had pleaded for the world, first by continent and then by national and tribal detail, was extended to an hour and a half, and made to include supplications in

behalf of the possible peoples in the several planets.
Everybody was pleased with this; everybody said,
"Now *this* is something *like*." By command, the
usual three-hour sermons were doubled in length.
The nation came in a body to testify their gratitude
to the new magistrate. The old law forbidding
cooking on the Sabbath was extended to the pro-
hibition of eating, also. By command, Sunday-
school was privileged to spread over into the week.
The joy of all classes was complete. In one short
month the new magistrate had become the people's
idol!

The time was ripe for this man's next move. He
began, cautiously at first, to poison the public mind
against England. He took the chief citizens aside,
one by one, and conversed with them on this topic.
Presently he grew bolder, and spoke out. He said
the nation owed it to itself, to its honor, to its great
traditions, to rise in its might and throw off "this
galling English yoke."

But the simple islanders answered:

"We had not noticed that it galled. How does
it gall? England sends a ship once in three or four
years to give us soap and clothing, and things which
we sorely need and gratefully receive; but she never
troubles us; she lets us go our own way."

"She lets you go your own way! So slaves have
felt and spoken in all the ages! This speech shows
how fallen you are, how base, how brutalized you
have become, under this grinding tyranny! What!
has all manly pride forsaken you? Is liberty nothing? Are you content to be a mere appendage

to a foreign and hateful sovereignty, when you might rise up and take your rightful place in the august family of nations, great, free, enlightened, independent, the minion of no sceptered master, but the arbiter of your own destiny, and a voice and a power in decreeing the destinies of your sister-sovereignties of the world?"

Speeches like this produced an effect by and by. Citizens began to feel the English yoke; they did not know exactly how or whereabouts they felt it, but they were perfectly certain they did feel it. They got to grumbling a good deal, and chafing under their chains, and longing for relief and release. They presently fell to hating the English flag, that sign and symbol of their nation's degradation; they ceased to glance up at it as they passed the capitol, but averted their eyes and grated their teeth; and one morning, when it was found trampled into the mud at the foot of the staff, they left it there, and no man put his hand to it to hoist it again. A certain thing which was sure to happen sooner or later happened now. Some of the chief citizens went to the magistrate by night, and said:

"We can endure this hated tyranny no longer. How can we cast it off?"

"By a *coup d'état*."

"How?"

"A *coup d'état*. It is like this: everything is got ready, and at the appointed moment I, as the official head of the nation, publicly and solemnly proclaim its independence, and absolve it from allegiance to any and all other powers whatsoever."

"That sounds simple and easy. We can do that right away. Then what will be the next thing to do?"

"Seize all the defenses and public properties of all kinds, establish martial law, put the army and navy on a war footing, and proclaim the empire!"

This fine program dazzled these innocents. They said:

"This is grand—this is splendid; but will not England resist?"

"Let her. This rock is a Gibraltar."

"True. But about the empire? Do we *need* an empire and an emperor?"

"What you *need*, my friends, is unification. Look at Germany; look at Italy. They are unified. Unification is the thing. It makes living dear. That constitutes progress. We must have a standing army and a navy. Taxes follow, as a matter of course. All these things summed up make grandeur. With unification and grandeur, what more can you want? Very well—only the empire can confer these boons."

So on the 8th day of December Pitcairn's Island was proclaimed a free and independent nation; and on the same day the solemn coronation of Butterworth I., Emperor of Pitcairn's Island, took place, amid great rejoicings and festivities. The entire nation, with the exception of fourteen persons, mainly little children, marched past the throne in single file, with banners and music, the procession being upward of ninety feet long; and some said it was as much as three-quarters of a minute passing a given point. Nothing like it had ever been seen in

the history of the island before. Public enthusiasm was measureless.

Now straightway imperial reforms began. Orders of nobility were instituted. A minister of the navy was appointed, and the whale-boat put in commission. A minister of war was created, and ordered to proceed at once with the formation of a standing army. A first lord of the treasury was named, and commanded to get up a taxation scheme, and also open negotiations for treaties, offensive, defensive, and commercial, with foreign powers. Some generals and admirals were appointed; also some chamberlains, some equerries in waiting, and some lords of the bedchamber.

At this point all the material was used up. The Grand Duke of Galilee, minister of war, complained that all the sixteen grown men in the empire had been given great offices, and consequently would not consent to serve in the ranks; wherefore his standing army was at a standstill. The Marquis of Ararat, minister of the navy, made a similar complaint. He said he was willing to steer the whale-boat himself, but he *must* have somebody to man her.

The emperor did the best he could in the circumstances: he took all the boys above the age of ten years away from their mothers, and pressed them into the army, thus constructing a corps of seventeen privates, officered by one lieutenant-general and two major-generals. This pleased the minister of war, but procured the enmity of all the mothers in the land; for they said their precious ones must now find bloody graves in the fields of war, and he would be answerable for it. Some of the more heartbroken and unappeasable among them lay constantly in wait for the emperor and threw yams at him, unmindful of the body-guard.

On account of the extreme scarcity of material, it was found necessary to require the Duke of Bethany, postmaster-general, to pull stroke-oar in the navy, and thus sit in the rear of a noble of lower degree, namely, Viscount Canaan, lord justice of the common pleas. This turned the Duke of Bethany into a tolerably open malcontent and a secret conspirator —a thing which the emperor foresaw, but could not help.

Things went from bad to worse. The emperor raised Nancy Peters to the peerage on one day, and married her the next, notwithstanding, for reasons of state, the cabinet had strenuously advised him to marry Emmeline, eldest daughter of the Archbishop of Bethlehem. This caused trouble in a powerful quarter—the church. The new empress secured the support and friendship of two-thirds of the thirty-six grown women in the nation by absorbing them into her court as maids of honor; but this made deadly enemies of the remaining twelve. The families of the maids of honor soon began to rebel, because there was nobody at home to keep house. The twelve snubbed women refused to enter the imperial kitchen as servants; so the empress had to require the Countess of Jericho and other great court dames to fetch water, sweep the palace, and perform other menial and equally distasteful services. This made bad blood in that department.

Everybody fell to complaining that the taxes levied
for the support of the army, the navy, and the rest
of the imperial establishment were intolerably bur-
densome, and were reducing the nation to beggary.
The emperor's reply—"Look at Germany; look at
Italy. Are you better than they? and haven't you
unification?"—did not satisfy them. They said,
"People can't *eat* unification, and we are starving.
Agriculture has ceased. Everybody is in the army,
everybody is in the navy, everybody is in the public
service, standing around in a uniform, with nothing
whatever to do, nothing to eat, and nobody to till
the fields—"

"Look at Germany; look at Italy. It is the same
there. Such is unification, and there's no other way
to get it—no other way to keep it after you've got
it," said the poor emperor always.

But the grumblers only replied, "We can't *stand*
the taxes—we can't *stand* them."

Now right on top of this the cabinet reported a
national debt amounting to upward of forty-five
dollars—half a dollar to every individual in the
nation. And they proposed to fund something.
They had heard that this was always done in such
emergencies. They proposed duties on exports; also
on imports. And they wanted to issue bonds; also
paper money, redeemable in yams and cabbages in
fifty years. They said the pay of the army and of
the navy and of the whole governmental machine
was far in arrears, and unless something was done,
and done immediately, national bankruptcy must en-
sue, and possibly insurrection and revolution. The

emperor at once resolved upon a high - handed measure, and one of a nature never before heard of in Pitcairn's Island. He went in state to the church on Sunday morning, with the army at his back, and commanded the minister of the treasury to take up a collection.

That was the feather that broke the camel's back. First one citizen, and then another, rose and refused to submit to this unheard-of outrage—and each refusal was followed by the immediate confiscation of the malcontent's property. This vigor soon stopped the refusals, and the collection proceeded amid a sullen and ominous silence. As the emperor withdrew with the troops, he said, "I will teach you who is master here." Several persons shouted, "Down with unification!" They were at once arrested and torn from the arms of their weeping friends by the soldiery.

But in the mean time, as any prophet might have foreseen, a Social Democrat had been developed. As the emperor stepped into the gilded imperial wheelbarrow at the church door, the social democrat stabbed at him fifteen or sixteen times with a harpoon, but fortunately with such a peculiarly social democratic unprecision of aim as to do no damage.

That very night the convulsion came. The nation rose as one man—though forty-nine of the revolutionists were of the other sex. The infantry threw down their pitchforks; the artillery cast aside their cocoanuts; the navy revolted; the emperor was seized, and bound hand and foot in his palace. He was very much depressed. He said:

"I freed you from a grinding tyranny; I lifted you up out of your degradation, and made you a nation among nations; I gave you a strong, compact, centralized government; and, more than all, I gave you the blessing of blessings—unification. I have done all this, and my reward is hatred, insult, and these bonds. Take me; do with me as you will. I here resign my crown and all my dignities, and gladly do I release myself from their too heavy burden. For your sake I took them up; for your sake I lay them down. The imperial jewel is no more; now bruise and defile as ye will the useless setting."

By a unanimous voice the people condemned the ex-emperor and the social democrat to perpetual banishment from church services, or to perpetual labor as galley-slaves in the whale-boat—whichever they might prefer. The next day the nation assembled again, and rehoisted the British flag, reinstated the British tyranny, reduced the nobility to the condition of commoners again, and then straightway turned their diligent attention to the weeding of the ruined and neglected yam patches, and the rehabilitation of the old useful industries and the old healing and solacing pieties. The ex-emperor restored the lost trespass law, and explained that he had stolen it —not to injure any one, but to further his political projects. Therefore the nation gave the late chief magistrate his office again, and also his alienated property.

Upon reflection, the ex-emperor and the social democrat chose perpetual banishment from religious services in preference to perpetual labor as galley-slaves "*with* perpetual religious services," as they phrased it; wherefore the people believed that the poor fellows' troubles had unseated their reason, and so they judged it best to confine them for the present. Which they did.

Such is the history of Pitcairn's "doubtful acquisition."

THE CANVASSER'S TALE

POOR, sad-eyed stranger! There was that about his humble mien, his tired look, his decayed-gentility clothes, that almost reached the mustard-seed of charity that still remained, remote and lonely, in the empty vastness of my heart, notwithstanding I observed a portfolio under his arm, and said to myself, Behold, Providence hath delivered his servant into the hands of another canvasser.

Well, these people always get one interested. Before I well knew how it came about, this one was telling me his history, and I was all attention and sympathy. He told it something like this:

My parents died, alas, when I was a little, sinless child. My uncle Ithuriel took me to his heart and reared me as his own. He was my only relative in the wide world; but he was good and rich and generous. He reared me in the lap of luxury. I knew no want that money could satisfy.

In the fullness of time I was graduated, and went with two of my servants—my chamberlain and my valet—to travel in foreign countries. During four years I flitted upon careless wing amid the beauteous gardens of the distant strand, if you will permit this form of speech in one whose tongue was ever attuned to poesy; and indeed I so speak with confidence, as one unto his kind, for I perceive by your eyes that you too, sir, are gifted with the divine inflation. In those far lands I reveled in the ambrosial food that fructifies the soul, the mind, the heart. But of all things, that which most appealed to my inborn esthetic taste was the prevailing custom there, among the rich, of making collections of elegant and costly rarities, dainty *objets de vertu*, and in an evil hour I tried to uplift my uncle Ithuriel to a plane of sympathy with this exquisite employment.

I wrote and told him of one gentleman's vast collection of shells; another's noble collection of meerschaum pipes; another's elevating and refining collection of undecipherable autographs; another's priceless collection of old china; another's enchanting collection of postage-stamps—and so forth and so on. Soon my letters yielded fruit. My uncle began to look about for something to make a collection of. You may know, perhaps, how fleetly a taste like this dilates. His soon became a raging fever, though I knew it not. He began to neglect his great pork business; presently he wholly retired and turned an elegant leisure into a rabid search for curious things. His wealth was vast, and he spared it not. First he tried cow-bells. He made a collection which filled five large *salons*, and comprehended all the different sorts of cow-bells that ever had been contrived, save one. That one—an antique, and the only specimen extant—was possessed by another collector. My uncle offered enormous sums for it, but the gentleman would not sell. Doubtless you know what necessarily resulted. A true collector attaches no value to a collection that is not complete. His great heart breaks, he sells his hoard, he turns his mind to some field that seems unoccupied.

Thus did my uncle. He next tried brickbats. After piling up a vast and intensely interesting collection, the former difficulty supervened; his great heart broke again; he sold out his soul's idol to the retired brewer who possessed the missing brick. Then he tried flint hatchets and other implements of Primeval Man, but by and by discovered that the factory where they were made was supplying other collectors as well as himself. He tried Aztec inscriptions and stuffed whales—another failure, after incredible labor and expense. When his collection seemed at last perfect, a stuffed whale arrived from Greenland and an Aztec inscription from the Cundurango regions of Central America that made all former specimens insignificant. My uncle hastened to secure these noble gems. He got the stuffed whale, but another collector got the inscription. A real Cundurango, as possibly you know, is a possession of such supreme value that, when once a collector gets it, he will rather part with his family than with it. So my uncle sold out, and saw his darlings go forth, never more to return; and his coal-black hair turned white as snow in a single night.

Now he waited, and thought. He knew another disappointment might kill him. He was resolved that he would choose things next time that no other man was collecting. He carefully made up his mind, and once more entered the field—this time to make a collection of echoes.

"Of what?" said I.

Echoes, sir. His first purchase was an echo in Georgia that repeated four times; his next was a six-repeater in Maryland; his next was a thirteen-repeater in Maine; his next was a nine-repeater in Kansas; his next was a twelve-repeater in Tennessee, which he got cheap, so to speak, because it was out of repair, a portion of the crag which reflected it having tumbled down. He believed he could repair it at a cost of a few thousand dollars, and, by increasing the elevation with masonry, treble the repeating capacity; but the architect who undertook the job had never built an echo before, and so he utterly spoiled this one. Before he meddled with it, it used to talk back like a mother-in-law, but now it was only fit for the deaf-and-dumb asylum. Well, next he bought a lot of cheap little double-barreled echoes, scattered around over various states and territories; he got them at twenty per cent. off by taking the lot. Next he bought a perfect Gatling-gun of an echo in Oregon, and it cost a fortune, I can tell you. You may know, sir, that in the echo market the scale of prices is cumulative, like the carat-scale in diamonds; in fact, the same phraseology is used. A single-carat echo is worth but ten dollars over and above the value of the land it is on; a two-carat or double-barreled echo is worth thirty dollars; a five-carat is worth nine hundred and fifty; a ten-carat is worth thirteen thousand. My uncle's Oregon echo, which he called the Great Pitt Echo, was a twenty-two carat gem, and cost two hundred and sixteen thousand dollars—they threw the land in, for it was four hundred miles from a settlement.

Well, in the mean time my path was a path of roses. I was the accepted suitor of the only and lovely daughter of an English earl, and was beloved to distraction. In that dear presence I swam in seas of bliss. The family were content, for it was known that I was sole heir to an uncle held to be worth five millions of dollars. However, none of us knew that my uncle had become a collector, at least in anything more than a small way, for esthetic amusement.

Now gathered the clouds above my unconscious head. That divine echo, since known throughout the world as the Great Koh-i-noor, or Mountain of Repetitions, was discovered. It was a sixty-five-carat gem. You could utter a word and it would talk back at you for fifteen minutes, when the day was otherwise quiet. But behold, another fact came to light at the same time: another echo-collector was in the field. The two rushed to make the peerless purchase. The property consisted of a couple of small hills with a shallow swale between, out yonder among the back settlements of New York State. Both men arrived on the ground at the same time, and neither knew the other was there. The echo was not all owned by one man; a person by the name of Williamson Bolivar Jarvis owned the east hill, and a person by the name of Harbison J. Bledso owned the west hill; the swale between was the dividing-line. So while my uncle was buying Jarvis's hill for three million two hundred and eighty-five thousand dollars, the other party was buying Bledso's hill for a shade over three million.

Now, do you perceive the natural result? Why, the noblest collection of echoes on earth was forever and ever incomplete, since it possessed but the one-half of the king echo of the universe. Neither man was content with this divided ownership, yet neither would sell to the other. There were jawings, bickerings, heart-burnings. And at last that other collector, with a malignity which only a collector can ever feel toward a man and a brother, proceeded to cut down his hill!

You see, as long as he could not have the echo, he was resolved that nobody should have it. He would remove his hill, and then there would be nothing to reflect my uncle's echo. My uncle remonstrated with him, but the man said, "I own one end of this echo; I choose to kill my end; you must take care of your own end yourself."

Well, my uncle got an injunction put on him. The other man appealed and fought it in a higher court. They carried it on up, clear to the Supreme Court of the United States. It made no end of trouble there. Two of the judges believed that an echo was personal property, because it was impalpable to sight and touch, and yet was purchasable, salable, and consequently taxable; two others believed that an echo was real estate, because it was manifestly attached to the land, and was not removable from place to place; other of the judges contended that an echo was not property at all.

It was finally decided that the echo was property;

that the hills were property; that the two men were separate and independent owners of the two hills, but tenants in common in the echo; therefore defendant was at full liberty to cut down his hill, since it belonged solely to him, but must give bonds in three million dollars as indemnity for damages which might result to my uncle's half of the echo. This decision also debarred my uncle from using defendant's hill to reflect his part of the echo, without defendant's consent; he must use only his own hill; if his part of the echo would not go, under these circumstances, it was sad, of course, but the court could find no remedy. The court also debarred defendant from using my uncle's hill to reflect *his* end of the echo, without consent. You see the grand result! Neither man would give consent, and so that astonishing and most noble echo had to cease from its great powers; and since that day that magnificent property is tied up and unsalable.

A week before my wedding-day, while I was still swimming in bliss and the nobility were gathering from far and near to honor our espousals, came news of my uncle's death, and also a copy of his will, making me his sole heir. He was gone; alas, my dear benefactor was no more. The thought surcharges my heart even at this remote day. I handed the will to the earl; I could not read it for the blinding tears. The earl read it; then he sternly said, "Sir, do you call this wealth?—but doubtless you do in your inflated country. Sir, you are left sole heir to a vast collection of echoes—if a thing can be called a collection that is scattered far and wide over the huge length and breadth of the American continent; sir, this is not all; you are head and ears in debt; there is not an echo in the lot but has a mortgage on it; sir, I am not a hard man, but I must look to my child's interest; if you had but one echo which you could honestly call your own, if you had but one echo which was free from incumbrance, so that you could retire to it with my child, and by humble, painstaking industry cultivate and improve it, and thus wrest from it a maintenance, I would not say you nay; but I cannot marry my child to a beggar. Leave his side, my darling; go, sir, take your mortgage-ridden echoes and quit my sight forever.''

My noble Celestine clung to me in tears, with loving arms, and swore she would willingly, nay gladly, marry me, though I had not an echo in the world. But it could not be. We were torn asunder, she to pine and die within the twelvemonth, I to toil life's long journey sad and alone, praying daily, hourly, for that release which shall join us together again in that dear realm where the wicked cease from troubling and the weary are at rest. Now, sir, if you will be so kind as to look at these maps and plans in my portfolio, I am sure I can sell you an echo for less money than any man in the trade. Now this one, which cost my uncle ten dollars, thirty years ago, and is one of the sweetest things in Texas, I will let you have for—

''Let me interrupt you,'' I said. ''My friend, I have not had a moment's respite from canvassers this day. I have bought a sewing-machine which I did not want; I have bought a map which is mistaken in all its details; I have bought a clock which will not go; I have bought a moth poison which the moths prefer to any other beverage; I have bought no end of useless inventions, and now I have had enough of this foolishness. I would not have one of your echoes if you were even to give it to me. I would not let it stay on the place. I always hate a man that tries to sell me echoes. You see this gun? Now take your collection and move on; let us not have bloodshed."

But he only smiled a sad, sweet smile, and got out some more diagrams. You know the result perfectly well, because you know that when you have once opened the door to a canvasser, the trouble is done and you have got to suffer defeat.

I compromised with this man at the end of an intolerable hour. I bought two double-barreled echoes in good condition, and he threw in another, which he said was not salable because it only spoke German. He said, "She was a perfect polyglot once, but somehow her palate got down."

AN ENCOUNTER WITH AN
INTERVIEWER

THE nervous, dapper, "peart" young man took
the chair I offered him, and said he was con-
nected with the *Daily Thunderstorm*, and added:

"Hoping it's no harm, I've come to interview you."

"Come to what?"

"*Interview* you."

"Ah! I see. Yes—yes. Um! Yes—yes."

I was not feeling bright that morning. Indeed,
my powers seemed a bit under a cloud. However,
I went to the bookcase, and when I had been looking
six or seven minutes I found I was obliged to refer
to the young man. I said:

"How do you spell it?"

"Spell what?"

"Interview."

"Oh, my goodness! what do you want to spell
it for?"

"I don't want to spell it; I want to see what it
means."

"Well, this is astonishing, I must say. *I* can tell
you what it means, if you—if you—"

"Oh, all right! That will answer, and much
obliged to you, too."

"In, *in*, ter, *ter*, *inter*—"

"Then you spell it with an *I?*"

"Why, certainly!"

"Oh, that is what took me so long."

"Why, my *dear* sir, what did *you* propose to spell it with?"

"Well, I—I—hardly know. I had the Unabridged, and I was ciphering around in the back end, hoping I might tree her among the pictures. But it's a very old edition."

"Why, my friend, they wouldn't have a *picture* of it in even the latest e— My dear sir, I beg your pardon, I mean no harm in the world, but you do not look as—as—intelligent as I had expected you would. No harm—I mean no harm at all."

"Oh, don't mention it! It has often been said, and by people who would not flatter and who could have no inducement to flatter, that I am quite remarkable in that way. Yes—yes; they always speak of it with rapture."

"I can easily imagine it. But about this interview. You know it is the custom, now, to interview any man who has become notorious."

"Indeed, I had not heard of it before. It must be very interesting. What do you do it with?"

"Ah, well—well—well—this is disheartening. It *ought* to be done with a club in some cases; but customarily it consists in the interviewer asking questions and the interviewed answering them. It is all the rage now. Will you let me ask you certain questions calculated to bring out the salient points of your public and private history?"

"Oh, with pleasure—with pleasure. I have a very

bad memory, but I hope you will not mind that. That is to say, it is an irregular memory—singularly irregular. Sometimes it goes in a gallop, and then again it will be as much as a fortnight passing a given point. This is a great grief to me."

"Oh, it is no matter, so you will try to do the best you can."

"I will. I will put my whole mind on it."

"Thanks. Are you ready to begin?"

"Ready."

Q. How old are you?

A. Nineteen, in June.

Q. Indeed. I would have taken you to be thirty-five or six. Where were you born?

A. In Missouri.

Q. When did you begin to write?

A. In 1836.

Q. Why, how could that be, if you are only nineteen now?

A. I don't know. It does seem curious, somehow.

Q. It does, indeed. Whom do you consider the most remarkable man you ever met?

A. Aaron Burr.

Q. But you never could have met Aaron Burr, if you are only nineteen years—

A. Now, if you know more about me than I do, what do you ask me for?

Q. Well, it was only a suggestion; nothing more. How did you happen to meet Burr?

A. Well, I happened to be at his funeral one day, and he asked me to make less noise, and—

Q. But, good heavens! if you were at his funeral,

he must have been dead, and if he was dead how could he care whether you made a noise or not?

A. I don't know. He was always a particular kind of a man that way.

Q. Still, I don't understand it at all. You say he spoke to you, and that he was dead.

A. I didn't say he was dead.

Q. But wasn't he dead?

A. Well, some said he was, some said he wasn't.

Q. What did you think?

A. Oh, it was none of my business! It wasn't any of my funeral.

Q. Did you— However, we can never get this matter straight. Let me ask about something else. What was the date of your birth?

A. Monday, October 31, 1693.

Q. What! Impossible! That would make you a hundred and eighty years old. How do you account for that?

A. I don't account for it at all.

Q. But you said at first you were only nineteen, and now you make yourself out to be one hundred and eighty. It is an awful discrepancy.

A. Why, have you noticed that? (Shaking hands.) Many a time it has seemed to me like a discrepancy, but somehow I couldn't make up my mind. How quick you notice a thing!

Q. Thank you for the compliment, as far as it goes. Had you, or have you, any brothers or sisters?

A. Eh! I—I—I think so—yes—but I don't remember.

Q. Well, that is the most extraordinary statement I ever heard!

A. Why, what makes you think that?

Q. How could I think otherwise? Why, look here! Who is this a picture of on the wall? Isn't that a brother of yours?

A. Oh, yes, yes, yes! Now you remind me of it; that *was* a brother of mine. That's William—*Bill* we called him. Poor old Bill!

Q. Why? Is he dead, then?

A. Ah! well, I suppose so. We never could tell. There was a great mystery about it.

Q. That is sad, very sad. He disappeared, then?

A. Well, yes, in a sort of general way. We buried him.

Q. *Buried* him! *Buried* him, without knowing whether he was dead or not?

A. Oh, no! Not that. He was dead enough.

Q. Well, I confess that I can't understand this. If you buried him, and you knew he was dead—

A. No! no! We only thought he was.

Q. Oh, I see! He came to life again?

A. I bet he didn't.

Q. Well, I never heard anything like this. *Somebody* was dead. *Somebody* was buried. Now, where was the mystery?

A. Ah! that's just it! That's it exactly. You see, we were twins—defunct and I—and we got mixed in the bathtub when we were only two weeks old, and one of us was drowned. But we didn't know which. Some think it was Bill. Some think it was me.

Q. Well, that *is* remarkable. What do *you* think?

A. Goodness knows! I would give whole worlds to know. This solemn, this awful mystery has cast a gloom over my whole life. But I will tell you a secret now, which I never have revealed to any creature before. One of us had a peculiar mark—a large mole on the back of his left hand; that was *me*. *That child was the one that was drowned!*

Q. Very well, then, I don't see that there is any mystery about it, after all.

A. You don't? Well, *I* do. Anyway, I don't see how they could ever have been such a blundering lot as to go and bury the wrong child. But, 'sh!— don't mention it where the family can hear of it. Heaven knows they have heartbreaking troubles enough without adding this.

Q. Well, I believe I have got material enough for the present, and I am very much obliged to you for the pains you have taken. But I was a good deal interested in that account of Aaron Burr's funeral. Would you mind telling me what particular circumstance it was that made you think Burr was such a remarkable man?

A. Oh! it was a mere trifle! Not one man in fifty would have noticed it at all. When the sermon was over, and the procession all ready to start for the cemetery, and the body all arranged nice in the hearse, he said he wanted to take a last look at the scenery, and so he *got up and rode with the driver*.

Then the young man reverently withdrew. He was very pleasant company, and I was sorry to see him go.

PARIS NOTES[1]

THE Parisian travels but little, he knows no language but his own, reads no literature but his own, and consequently he is pretty narrow and pretty self-sufficient. However, let us not be too sweeping; there are Frenchmen who know languages not their own: these are the waiters. Among the rest, they know English; that is, they know it on the European plan—which is to say, they can speak it, but can't understand it. They easily make themselves understood, but it is next to impossible to word an English sentence in such a way as to enable them to comprehend it. They think they comprehend it; they pretend they do; but they don't. Here is a conversation which I had with one of these beings; I wrote it down at the time, in order to have it exactly correct.

I. These are fine oranges.   Where are they grown?

He. More?   Yes, I will bring them.

I. No, do not bring any more; I only want to know where they are from—where they are raised.

He. Yes? (with imperturbable mien and rising inflection.)

I. Yes.   Can you tell me what country they are from?

---

[1] Crowded out of "A Tramp Abroad" to make room for more vital statistics.—M. T.

He. Yes? (blandly, with rising inflection.)

I (disheartened). They are very nice.

He. Good night. (Bows, and retires, quite satisfied with himself.)

That young man could have become a good English scholar by taking the right sort of pains, but he was French, and wouldn't do that. How different is the case with our people; they utilize every means that offers. There are some alleged French Protestants in Paris, and they built a nice little church on one of the great avenues that lead away from the Arch of Triumph, and proposed to listen to the correct thing, preached in the correct way, there, in their precious French tongue, and be happy. But their little game does not succeed. Our people are always there ahead of them Sundays, and take up all the room. When the minister gets up to preach, he finds his house full of devout foreigners, each ready and waiting, with his little book in his hand —a morocco-bound Testament, apparently. But only apparently; it is Mr. Bellows's admirable and exhaustive little French-English dictionary, which in look and binding and size is just like a Testament— and those people are there to study French. The building has been nicknamed "The Church of the Gratis French Lesson."

These students probably acquire more language than general information, for I am told that a French sermon is like a French speech—it never names a historical event, but only the date of it; if you are not up in dates, you get left. A French speech is something like this:

Comrades, citizens, brothers, noble parts of the only sublime and perfect nation, let us not forget that the 21st January cast off our chains; that the 10th August relieved us of the shameful presence of foreign spies; that the 5th September was its own justification before heaven and humanity; that the 18th Brumaire contained the seeds of its own punishment; that the 14th July was the mighty voice of liberty proclaiming the resurrection, the new day, and inviting the oppressed peoples of the earth to look upon the divine face of France and live; and let us here record our everlasting curse against the man of the 2d December, and declare in thunder tones, the native tones of France, that but for him there had been no 17th March in history, no 12th October, no 19th January, no 22d April, no 16th November, no 30th September, no 2d July, no 14th February, no 29th June, no 15th August, no 31st May—that but for him, France the pure, the grand, the peerless, had had a serene and vacant almanac to-day!

I have heard of one French sermon which closed in this odd yet eloquent way:

My hearers, we have sad cause to remember the man of the 13th January. The results of the vast crime of the 13th January have been in just proportion to the magnitude of the act itself. But for it there had been no 30th November—sorrowful spectacle! The grisly deed of the 16th June had not been done but for it, nor had the man of the 16th June known existence; to it alone the 3d September was due, also the fatal 12th October. Shall we, then, be grateful for the 13th January, with its freight of death for you and me and all that breathe? Yes, my friends, for it gave us also that which had never come but for it, and it alone—the blessed 25th December.

It may be well enough to explain, though in the case of many of my readers this will hardly be necessary. The man of the 13th January is Adam; the crime of that date was the eating of the apple; the sorrowful spectacle of the 30th November was the expulsion from Eden; the grisly deed of the 16th

June was the murder of Abel; the act of the 3d September was the beginning of the journey to the land of Nod; the 12th day of October, the last mountain-tops disappeared under the flood. When you go to church in France, you want to take your almanac with you—annotated.

LEGEND OF SAGENFELD, IN GERMANY[1]

I

MORE than a thousand years ago this small district was a kingdom—a little bit of a kingdom, a sort of dainty little toy kingdom, as one might say. It was far removed from the jealousies, strifes, and turmoils of that old warlike day, and so its life was a simple life, its people a gentle and guileless race; it lay always in a deep dream of peace, a soft Sabbath tranquillity; there was no malice, there was no envy, there was no ambition, consequently there were no heart-burnings, there was no unhappiness in the land.

In the course of time the old king died and his little son Hubert came to the throne. The people's love for him grew daily; he was so good and so pure and so noble, that by and by his love became a passion, almost a worship. Now at his birth the soothsayers had diligently studied the stars and found something written in that shining book to this effect:

In Hubert's fourteenth year a pregnant event will happen; the animal whose singing shall sound sweetest

[1] Left out of "A Tramp Abroad" because its authenticity seemed doubtful, and could not at that time be proved.—M. T.

*in Hubert's ear shall save Hubert's life. So long as the
king and the nation shall honor this animal's race for
this good deed, the ancient dynasty shall not fail of an
heir, nor the nation know war or pestilence or poverty.
But beware an erring choice!*

All through the king's thirteenth year but one
thing was talked of by the soothsayers, the states-
men, the little parliament, and the general people.
That one thing was this: How is the last sentence
of the prophecy to be understood? What goes before
seems to mean that the saving animal will choose
itself at the proper time; but the closing sentence
seems to mean that the *king* must choose beforehand,
and say what singer among the animals pleases him
best, and that if he choose wisely the chosen animal
will save his life, his dynasty, his people, but that if
he should make "an erring choice"—beware!

By the end of the year there were as many opinions
about this matter as there had been in the beginning;
but a majority of the wise and the simple were agreed
that the safest plan would be for the little king to
make choice beforehand, and the earlier the better.
So an edict was sent forth commanding all persons
who owned singing creatures to bring them to the
great hall of the palace in the morning of the first
day of the new year. This command was obeyed.
When everything was in readiness for the trial, the
king made his solemn entry with the great officers
of the crown, all clothed in their robes of state.
The king mounted his golden throne and prepared to
give judgment. But he presently said:

"These creatures all sing at once; the noise is unendurable; no one can choose in such a turmoil. Take them all away, and bring back one at a time."

This was done. One sweet warbler after another charmed the young king's ear and was removed to make way for another candidate. The precious minutes slipped by; among so many bewitching songsters he found it hard to choose, and all the harder because the promised penalty for an error was so terrible that it unsettled his judgment and made him afraid to trust his own ears. He grew nervous and his face showed distress. His ministers saw this, for they never took their eyes from him a moment. Now they began to say in their hearts:

"He has lost courage—the cool head is gone—he will err—he and his dynasty and his people are doomed!"

At the end of an hour the king sat silent awhile, and then said:

"Bring back the linnet."

The linnet trilled forth her jubilant music. In the midst of it the king was about to uplift his scepter in sign of choice, but checked himself and said:

"But let us be sure. Bring back the thrush; let them sing together."

The thrush was brought, and the two birds poured out their marvels of song together. The king wavered, then his inclination began to settle and strengthen—one could see it in his countenance. Hope budded in the hearts of the old ministers, their pulses began to beat quicker, the scepter began to rise slowly, when: There was a hideous interruption! It was a sound like this—just at the door:

"Waw . . . *he!* waw . . . *he!*—waw-he!—waw-he!—waw-he!"

Everybody was sorely startled—and enraged at himself for showing it.

The next instant the dearest, sweetest, prettiest little peasant-maid of nine years came tripping in, her brown eyes glowing with childish eagerness; but when she saw that august company and those angry faces she stopped and hung her head and put her poor coarse apron to her eyes. Nobody gave her welcome, none pitied her. Presently she looked up timidly through her tears, and said:

"My lord the king, I pray you pardon me, for I meant no wrong. I have no father and no mother, but I have a goat and a donkey, and they are all in all to me. My goat gives me the sweetest milk, and when my dear good donkey brays it seems to me there is no music like to it. So when my lord the king's jester said the sweetest singer among all the animals should save the crown and nation, and moved me to bring him here—"

All the court burst into a rude laugh, and the child fled away crying, without trying to finish her speech. The chief minister gave a private order that she and her disastrous donkey be flogged beyond the precincts of the palace and commanded to come within them no more.

Then the trial of the birds was resumed. The two birds sang their best, but the scepter lay motionless in the king's hand. Hope died slowly out in the breasts of all. An hour went by; two hours, still no decision. The day waned to its close, and the waiting multitudes outside the palace grew crazed with anxiety and apprehension. The twilight came on, the shadows fell deeper and deeper. The king and his court could no longer see each other's faces. No one spoke—none called for lights. The great trial had been made; it had failed; each and all wished to hide their faces from the light and cover up their deep trouble in their own hearts.

Finally—hark! A rich, full strain of the divinest melody streamed forth from a remote part of the hall—the nightingale's voice!

"Up!" shouted the king, "let all the bells make proclamation to the people, for the choice is made and we have not erred. King, dynasty, and nation are saved. From henceforth let the nightingale be honored throughout the land forever. And publish it among all the people that whosoever shall insult a nightingale, or injure it, shall suffer death. The king hath spoken."

All that little world was drunk with joy. The castle and the city blazed with bonfires all night long, the people danced and drank and sang, and the triumphant clamor of the bells never ceased.

From that day the nightingale was a sacred bird. Its song was heard in every house; the poets wrote its praises; the painters painted it; its sculptured image adorned every arch and turret and fountain and public building. It was even taken into the king's councils; and no grave matter of state was decided until the soothsayers had laid the thing before the state nightingale and translated to the ministry what it was that the bird had sung about it.

II

THE young king was very fond of the chase. When the summer was come he rode forth with hawk and hound, one day, in a brilliant company of his nobles. He got separated from them by and by, in a great forest, and took what he imagined a near cut, to find them again; but it was a mistake. He rode on and on, hopefully at first, but with sinking courage finally. Twilight came on, and still he was plunging through a lonely and unknown land. Then came a catastrophe. In the dim light he forced his horse through a tangled thicket overhanging a steep and rocky declivity. When horse and rider reached the bottom, the former had a broken neck and the latter a broken leg. The poor little king lay there suffering agonies of pain, and each hour seemed a long month to him. He kept his ear strained to hear any sound that might promise hope of rescue; but he heard no voice, no sound of horn or bay of hound. So at last he gave up all hope, and said, "Let death come, for come it must."

Just then the deep, sweet song of a nightingale swept across the still wastes of the night.

"Saved!" the king said. "Saved! It is the sacred bird, and the prophecy is come true. The gods themselves protected me from error in the choice."

He could hardly contain his joy; he could not

word his gratitude. Every few moments now he thought he caught the sound of approaching succor. But each time it was a disappointment; no succor came. The dull hours drifted on. Still no help came—but still the sacred bird sang on. He began to have misgivings about his choice, but he stifled them. Toward dawn the bird ceased. The morning came, and with it thirst and hunger; but no succor. The day waxed and waned. At last the king cursed the nightingale.

Immediately the song of the thrush came from out the wood. The king said in his heart, "This was the true bird—my choice was false—succor will come now."

But it did not come. Then he lay many hours insensible. When he came to himself, a linnet was singing. He listened—with apathy. His faith was gone. "These birds," he said, "can bring no help; I and my house and my people are doomed." He turned him about to die; for he was grown very feeble from hunger and thirst and suffering, and felt that his end was near. In truth, he wanted to die, and be released from pain. For long hours he lay without thought or feeling or motion. Then his senses returned. The dawn of the third morning was breaking. Ah, the world seemed very beautiful to those worn eyes. Suddenly a great longing to live rose up in the lad's heart, and from his soul welled a deep and fervent prayer that Heaven would have mercy upon him and let him see his home and his friends once more. In that instant a soft, a faint, a far-off sound, but oh, how inexpressibly sweet to his waiting ear, came floating out of the distance:

"Waw . . . *he!* waw . . . *he!* waw-he!—waw-he!
—waw-he!"

"*That*, oh, *that* song is sweeter, a thousand times
sweeter than the voice of the nightingale, thrush, or
linnet, for it brings not mere hope, but *certainty* of
succor; and now, indeed, am I saved! The sacred
singer has chosen itself, as the oracle intended; the
prophecy is fulfilled, and my life, my house, and my
people are redeemed. The ass shall be sacred from
this day!"

The divine music grew nearer and nearer, stronger
and stronger—and ever sweeter and sweeter to the
perishing sufferer's ear. Down the declivity the
docile little donkey wandered, cropping herbage and
singing as he went; and when at last he saw the dead
horse and the wounded king, he came and snuffed at
them with simple and marveling curiosity. The
king petted him, and he knelt down as had been his
wont when his little mistress desired to mount.
With great labor and pain the lad drew himself upon
the creature's back, and held himself there by aid
of the generous ears. The ass went singing forth
from the place and carried the king to the little
peasant-maid's hut. She gave him her pallet for a
bed, refreshed him with goat's milk, and then flew to
tell the great news to the first scouting-party of
searchers she might meet.

The king got well. His first act was to proclaim
the sacredness and inviolability of the ass; his second
was to add this particular ass to his cabinet and
make him chief minister of the crown; his third was
to have all the statues and effigies of nightingales

throughout his kingdom destroyed, and replaced by statues and effigies of the sacred donkey; and his fourth was to announce that when the little peasant-maid should reach her fifteenth year he would make her his queen—and he kept his word.

Such is the legend. This explains why the moldering image of the ass adorns all these old crumbling walls and arches; and it explains why, during many centuries, an ass was always the chief minister in that royal cabinet, just as is still the case in most cabinets to this day; and it also explains why, in that little kingdom, during many centuries, all great poems, all great speeches, all great books, all public solemnities, and all royal proclamations, always began with these stirring words:

"Waw . . . *he!* waw . . . *he!*—waw-he!—waw-he! —waw-he!"

SPEECH ON THE WEATHER

The next toast was: "The Oldest Inhabitant—The Weather
of New England."

> Who can lose it and forget it?
> Who can have it and regret it?
>
> Be interposer 'twixt us Twain.
> *Merchant of Venice.*

To this Samuel L. Clemens (Mark Twain) replied as follows:—

I REVERENTLY believe that the Maker who made us all makes everything in New England but the weather. I don't know who makes that, but I think it must be raw apprentices in the weather-clerk's factory who experiment and learn how, in New England, for board and clothes, and then are promoted to make weather for countries that require a good article, and will take their custom elsewhere if they don't get it. There is a sumptuous variety about the New England weather that compels the stranger's admiration—and regret. The weather is always doing something there; always attending strictly to business; always getting up new designs and trying them on the people to see how they will

go. But it gets through more business in spring than in any other season. In the spring I have counted one hundred and thirty-six different kinds of weather inside of four-and-twenty hours. It was I that made the fame and fortune of that man that had that marvelous collection of weather on exhibition at the Centennial, that so astounded the foreigners. He was going to travel all over the world and get specimens from all the climes. I said, "Don't you do it; you come to New England on a favorable spring day." I told him what we could do in the way of style, variety, and quantity. Well, he came and he made his collection in four days. As to variety, why, he confessed that he got hundreds of kinds of weather that he had never heard of before. And as to quantity—well, after he had picked out and discarded all that was blemished in any way, he not only had weather enough, but weather to spare; weather to hire out; weather to sell; to deposit; weather to invest; weather to give to the poor. The people of New England are by nature patient and forbearing, but there are some things which they will not stand. Every year they kill a lot of poets for writing about "Beautiful Spring." These are generally casual visitors, who bring their notions of spring from somewhere else, and cannot, of course, know how the natives feel about spring. And so the first thing they know the opportunity to inquire how they feel has permanently gone by. Old Probabilities has a mighty reputation for accurate prophecy, and thoroughly well deserves it. You take up the paper and observe how crisply and confidently he checks off what to-day's weather is going to be on the Pacific, down South, in the Middle States, in the Wisconsin region. See him sail along in the joy and pride of his power till he gets to New England, and then see his tail drop. *He* doesn't know what the weather is going to be in New England. Well, he mulls over it, and by and by he gets out something about like this: Probable northeast to southwest winds, varying to the southward and westward and eastward, and points between, high and low barometer swapping around from place to place; probable areas of rain, snow, hail, and drought, succeeded or preceded by earthquakes, with thunder and lightning. Then he jots down this postscript from his wandering mind, to cover accidents: "But it is possible that the program may be wholly changed in the mean time." Yes, one of the brightest gems in the New England weather is the dazzling uncertainty of it. There is only one thing certain about it: you are certain there is going to be plenty of it—a perfect grand review; but you never can tell which end of the procession is going to move first. You fix up for the drought; you leave your umbrella in the house and sally out, and two to one you get drowned. You make up your mind that the earthquake is due; you stand from under, and take hold of something to steady yourself, and the first thing you know you get struck by lightning. These are great disappointments; but they can't be helped. The lightning there is peculiar; it is so convincing, that when it strikes a thing it doesn't leave enough of that thing behind for you to tell whether— Well, you'd think it was something valuable, and a Congressman had been there. And the thunder. When the thunder begins to merely tune up and scrape and saw, and key up the instruments for the performance, strangers say, "Why, what awful thunder you have here!" But when the baton is raised and the real concert begins, you'll find that stranger down in the cellar with his head in the ash-barrel. Now as to the *size* of the weather in New England—lengthways, I mean. It is utterly disproportioned to the size of that little country. Half the time, when it is packed as full as it can stick, you will see that New England weather sticking out beyond the edges and projecting around hundreds and hundreds of miles over the neighboring states. She can't hold a tenth part of her weather. You can see cracks all about where she has strained herself trying to do it. I could speak volumes about the inhuman perversity of the New England weather, but I will give but a single specimen. I like to hear rain on a tin roof. So I covered part of my roof with tin, with an eye to that luxury. Well, sir, do you think it ever rains on that tin? No, sir; skips it every time. Mind, in this speech I have been trying merely to do honor to the New England weather—no language could do it justice. But, after all, there is at least one or two things about that weather (or, if you please, effects produced by it) which we residents would not like to part with. If we hadn't our bewitching autumn foliage, we should still have to credit the weather with one feature which compensates for all its bullying vagaries—the ice-storm: when a leafless tree is clothed with ice from the bottom to the top—ice that is as bright and clear as crystal; when every bough and twig is strung with ice-beads, frozen dewdrops, and the whole tree sparkles cold and white, like the Shah of Persia's diamond plume. Then the wind waves the branches and the sun comes out and turns all those myriads of beads and drops to prisms that glow and burn and flash with all manner of colored fires, which change and change again with inconceivable rapidity from blue to red, from red to green, and green to gold— the tree becomes a spraying fountain, a very explosion of dazzling jewels; and it stands there the acme, the climax, the supremest possibility in art or nature, of bewildering, intoxicating, intolerable magnificence. One cannot make the words too strong.

CONCERNING THE AMERICAN LANGUAGE[1]

THERE was an Englishman in our compartment, and he complimented me on—on what? But you would never guess. He complimented me on my English. He said Americans in general did not speak the English language as correctly as I did. I said I was obliged to him for his compliment, since I knew he meant it for one, but that I was not fairly entitled to it, for I did not speak English at all—I only spoke American.

He laughed, and said it was a distinction without a difference. I said no, the difference was not prodigious, but still it was considerable. We fell into a friendly dispute over the matter. I put my case as well as I could, and said:

"The languages were identical several generations ago, but our changed conditions and the spread of our people far to the south and far to the west have made many alterations in our pronunciation, and have introduced new words among us and changed the meanings of many old ones. English people talk through their noses; we do not. We say *know*, English people say *não*; we say *cow*, the Briton says *kãow*; we—"

[1] Being part of a chapter which was crowded out of "A Tramp Abroad."—M. T.

"Oh, come! that is pure Yankee; everybody knows that."

"Yes, it is pure Yankee; that is true. One cannot hear it in America outside of the little corner called New England, which is Yankee land. The English themselves planted it there, two hundred and fifty years ago, and there it remains; it has never spread. But England talks through her nose yet; the Londoner and the backwoods New-Englander pronounce 'know' and 'cow' alike, and then the Briton unconsciously satirizes himself by making fun of the Yankee's pronunciation."

We argued this point at some length; nobody won; but no matter, the fact remains—Englishmen say *nāo* and *kǎow* for "know" and "cow," and that is what the rustic inhabitant of a very small section of America does.

"You conferred your *a* upon New England, too, and there it remains; it has not traveled out of the narrow limits of those six little states in all these two hundred and fifty years. All England uses it, New England's small population—say four millions—use it, but we have forty-five millions who do not use it. You say 'glahs of wawtah,' so does New England; at least, New England says *glahs*. America at large flattens the *a*, and says 'glass of water.' These sounds are pleasanter than yours; you may think they are not right—well, in English they are *not* right, but in 'American' they are. You say *flahsk*, and *bahsket*, and *jackahss;* we say 'flask,' 'basket,' 'jackass'—sounding the *a* as it is in 'tallow,' 'fallow,' and so on. Up to as late as 1847 Mr. Webster's Dictionary had the impudence to still pronounce 'basket' *bahsket*, when he knew that outside of his little New England all America shortened the *a* and paid no attention to his English broadening of it. However, it called itself an English Dictionary, so it was proper enough that it should stick to English forms, perhaps. It still calls itself an English Dictionary today, but it has quietly ceased to pronounce 'basket' as if it were spelt *bahsket*. In the American language the *h* is respected; the *h* is not dropped or added improperly."

"The same is the case in England—I mean among the educated classes, of course."

"Yes, that is true; but a nation's language is a very large matter. It is not simply a manner of speech obtaining among the educated handful; the manner obtaining among the vast uneducated multitude must be considered also. Your uneducated masses speak English, you will not deny that; our uneducated masses speak American—it won't be fair for you to deny that, for you can see, yourself, that when your stable-boy says, 'It isn't the 'unting that 'urts the 'orse, but the 'ammer, 'ammer, 'ammer on the 'ard 'ighway,' and our stable-boy makes the same remark without suffocating a single *h*, these two people are manifestly talking two different languages. But if the signs are to be trusted, even your educated classes used to drop the *h*. They say *humble*, now, and *heroic*, and *historic*, etc., but I judge that they used to drop those *h*'s because your writers still keep up the fashion of putting *an* before those words, instead of *a*. This is what Mr. Darwin might call a 'rudimentary' sign that an *an* was justifiable once, and useful—when your educated classes used to say *'umble*, and *'eroic*, and *'istorical*. Correct writers of the American language do not put *an* before those words."

The English gentleman had something to say upon this matter, but never mind what he said—I'm not arguing his case. I have him at a disadvantage, now. I proceeded:

"In England you encourage an orator by exclaiming, 'H'yaah! h'yaah!' We pronounce it *heer* in some sections, 'h'*yer*' in others, and so on; but our whites do not say 'h'yaah,' pronouncing the *a*'s like the *a* in *ah*. I have heard English ladies say 'don't you'— making two separate and distinct words of it; your Mr. Burnand has satirized it. But we always say 'dontchu.' This is much better. Your ladies say, 'Oh, it's *o*ful nice!' Ours say, 'Oh, it's *aw*ful nice!' We say, '*Four* hundred,' you say '*For*'—as in the word *or*. Your clergymen speak of 'the Lawd,' ours of 'the Lord'; yours speak of 'the gawds of the heathen,' ours of 'the gods of the heathen.' When you are exhausted, you say you are 'knocked up.' We don't. When you say you will do a thing 'directly,' you mean 'immediately'; in the American language—generally speaking—the word signifies 'after a little.' When you say 'clever,' you mean 'capable'; with us the word used to mean 'accommodating,' but I don't know what it means now. Your word 'stout' means 'fleshy'; our word 'stout' usually means 'strong.' Your words 'gentleman' and 'lady' have a very restricted meaning; with us they include the barmaid, butcher, burglar, harlot, and horse-thief. You say, 'I haven't *got* any stockings on,' 'I haven't *got* any memory,' 'I haven't *got* any money in my purse'; we usually say, 'I haven't any stockings on,' 'I haven't any memory,' 'I haven't any money in my purse.' You say 'out of window'; we always put in a *the*. If one asks 'How old is that man?' the Briton answers, 'He will be about forty'; in the American language we should say, 'He *is* about forty.' However, I won't tire you, sir; but if I wanted to, I could pile up differences here until I not only convinced you that English and American are separate languages, but that when I speak my native tongue in its utmost purity an Englishman can't understand me at all."

"I don't wish to flatter you, but it is about all I can do to understand you *now*."

That was a very pretty compliment, and it put us on the pleasantest terms directly—I use the word in the English sense.

[*Later*—1882. Esthetes in many of our schools are now beginning to teach the pupils to broaden the *a*, and to say "don't you," in the elegant foreign way.]

ROGERS

THIS man Rogers happened upon me and introduced himself at the town of——, in the South of England, where I stayed awhile. His stepfather had married a distant relative of mine who was afterward hanged, and so he seemed to think a blood relationship existed between us. He came in every day and sat down and talked. Of all the bland, serene human curiosities I ever saw, I think he was the chiefest. He desired to look at my new chimney-pot hat. I was very willing, for I thought he would notice the name of the great Oxford Street hatter in it, and respect me accordingly. But he turned it about with a sort of grave compassion, pointed out two or three blemishes, and said that I, being so recently arrived, could not be expected to know where to supply myself. Said he would send me the address of *his* hatter. Then he said, "Pardon me," and proceeded to cut a neat circle of red tissue-paper; daintily notched the edges of it; took the mucilage and pasted it in my hat so as to cover the manufacturer's name. He said, "No one will know now where you got it. I will send you a hat-tip of my hatter, and you can paste it over this tissue circle." It was the calmest, coolest thing—I never admired a man so much in my life. Mind, he did this while his own hat sat offensively near our noses, on the table—an ancient extinguisher of the "slouch" pattern, limp and shapeless with age, discolored by vicissitudes of the weather, and banded by an equator of bear's grease that had stewed through.

Another time he examined my coat. I had no terrors, for over my tailor's door was the legend, "By Special Appointment Tailor to H. R. H. the Prince of Wales," etc. I did not know at the time that the most of the tailor shops had the same sign out, and that whereas it takes nine tailors to make an ordinary man, it takes a hundred and fifty to make a prince. He was full of compassion for my coat. Wrote down the address of his tailor for me. Did not tell me to mention my *nom de plume* and the tailor would put his best work on my garment, as complimentary people sometimes do, but said his tailor would hardly trouble himself for an unknown person (unknown person, when I thought I was so celebrated in England!—that was the cruelest cut), but cautioned me to mention *his* name, and it would be all right. Thinking to be facetious, I said:

"But he might sit up all night and injure his health."

"Well, *let* him," said Rogers; "I've done enough for him, for him to show some appreciation of it."

I might as well have tried to disconcert a mummy with my facetiousness. Said Rogers: "I get all my coats there — they're the only coats fit to be seen in."

I made one more attempt. I said, "I wish you had brought one with you—I would like to look at it."

"Bless your heart, haven't I got one on?—*this* article is Morgan's make."

I examined it. The coat had been bought ready-made, of a Chatham Street Jew, without any question—about 1848. It probably cost four dollars when it was new. It was ripped, it was frayed, it was napless and greasy. I could not resist showing him where it was ripped. It so affected him that I was almost sorry I had done it. First he seemed plunged into a bottomless abyss of grief. Then he roused himself, made a feint with his hands as if waving off the pity of a nation, and said—with what seemed to me a manufactured emotion—"No matter; no matter; don't mind me; do not bother about it. I can get another."

When he was thoroughly restored, so that he could examine the rip and command his feelings, he said, ah, *now* he understood it—his servant must have done it while dressing him that morning.

His servant! There was something awe-inspiring in effrontery like this.

Nearly every day he interested himself in some article of my clothing. One would hardly have expected this sort of infatuation in a man who always wore the same suit, and it a suit that seemed coeval with the Conquest.

It was an unworthy ambition, perhaps, but I *did* wish I could make this man admire *something* about me or something I did—you would have felt the same way. I saw my opportunity: I was about to return to London, and had "listed" my soiled linen for the wash. It made quite an imposing mountain in the corner of the room—fifty-four pieces. I hoped he would fancy it was the accumulation of a single week. I took up the wash-list, as if to see that it was all right, and then tossed it on the table, with pretended forgetfulness. Sure enough, he took it up and ran his eye along down to the grand total. Then he said, "You get off easy," and laid it down again.

His gloves were the saddest ruin, but he told me where I could get some like them. His shoes would hardly hold walnuts without leaking, but he liked to put his feet up on the mantelpiece and contemplate them. He wore a dim glass breastpin, which he called a "morphylitic diamond"—whatever that may mean—and said only two of them had ever been found—the Emperor of China had the other one.

Afterward, in London, it was a pleasure to me to see this fantastic vagabond come marching into the lobby of the hotel in his grand-ducal way, for he always had some new imaginary grandeur to develop —there was nothing stale about him but his clothes. If he addressed me when strangers were about, he always raised his voice a little and called me "Sir Richard," or "General," or "Your Lordship"—and when people began to stare and look deferential, he would fall to inquiring in a casual way why I disappointed the Duke of Argyll the night before; and then remind me of our engagement at the Duke of Westminster's for the following day. I think that for the time being these things were realities to him. He once came and invited me to go with him and spend the evening with the Earl of Warwick at his town house. I said I had received no formal invitation. He said that that was of no consequence, the Earl had no formalities for him or his friends. I asked if I could go just as I was. He said no, that would hardly do; evening dress was requisite at night in any gentleman's house. He said he would wait while I dressed, and then we would go to his apartments and I could take a bottle of champagne and a cigar while he dressed. I was very willing to see how this enterprise would turn out, so I dressed, and we started to his lodgings. He said if I didn't mind we would walk. So we tramped some four miles through the mud and fog, and finally found his "apartments"; they consisted of a single room over a barber's shop in a back street. Two chairs, a small table, an ancient valise, a wash-basin and pitcher (both on the floor in a corner), an unmade bed, a fragment of a looking-glass, and a flower-pot, with a perishing little rose geranium in it, which he called a century plant, and said it had not bloomed now for upward of two centuries—given to him by the late Lord Palmerston—(been offered a prodigious sum for it)—these were the contents of the room. Also a brass candlestick and a part of a candle. Rogers lit the candle, and told me to sit down and make myself at home. He said he hoped I was thirsty, because he would surprise my palate with an article of champagne that seldom got into a commoner's system; or would I prefer sherry, or port? Said he had port in bottles that were swathed in stratified cobwebs, every stratum representing a generation. And as for his cigars—well, I should judge of them myself. Then he put his head out at the door and called:

"Sackville!" No answer.

"Hi—Sackville!" No answer.

"Now what the devil can have become of that butler? I *never* allow a servant to— Oh, confound that idiot, he's got the *keys*. Can't get into the other rooms without the keys."

(I was just wondering at his intrepidity in still keeping up the delusion of the champagne, and trying to imagine how he was going to get out of the difficulty.)

Now he stopped calling Sackville and began to call "Anglesy." But Anglesy didn't come. He said, "This is the *second* time that that equerry has been absent without leave. To-morrow I'll discharge him."

Now he began to whoop for "Thomas," but Thomas didn't answer. Then for "Theodore," but no Theodore replied.

"Well, I give it up," said Rogers. "The servants never expect me at this hour, and so they're all off on a lark. Might get along without the equerry and the page, but can't have any wine or cigars without the butler, and can't dress without my valet."

I offered to help him dress, but he would not hear of it; and besides, he said he would not feel comfortable unless dressed by a practised hand. However, he finally concluded that he was such old friends with the Earl that it would not make any difference how he was dressed. So we took a cab, he gave the driver some directions, and we started. By and by we stopped before a large house and got out. I never had seen this man with a collar on. He now stepped under a lamp and got a venerable paper collar out of his coat pocket, along with a hoary cravat, and put them on. He ascended the stoop, and entered. Presently he reappeared, descended rapidly, and said:

"Come—quick!"

We hurried away, and turned the corner.

"Now we're safe," he said, and took off his collar and cravat and returned them to his pocket.

"Made a mighty narrow escape," said he.

"How?" said I.

"B' George, the Countess was there!"

"Well, what of that?—don't she know you?"

"Know me? Absolutely worships me. I just did happen to catch a glimpse of her before she saw me —and out I shot. Haven't seen her for two months —to rush in on her without any warning might have been fatal. She could *not* have stood it. I didn't know *she* was in town—thought she was at the castle. Let me lean on you—just a moment—there; now I am better—thank you; thank you ever so much. Lord bless me, what an escape!"

So I never got to call on the Earl, after all. But I marked the house for future reference. It proved to be an ordinary family hotel, with about a thousand plebeians roosting in it.

In most things Rogers was by no means a fool. In some things it was plain enough that he was a fool, but he certainly did not know it. He was in the "deadest" earnest in these matters. He died at sea, last summer, as the "Earl of Ramsgate."

THE LOVES OF ALONZO FITZ CLARENCE AND ROSANNAH ETHELTON

I

IT was well along in the forenoon of a bitter winter's day. The town of Eastport, in the state of Maine, lay buried under a deep snow that was newly fallen. The customary bustle in the streets was wanting. One could look long distances down them and see nothing but a dead-white emptiness, with silence to match. Of course I do not mean that you could *see* the silence—no, you could only hear it. The sidewalks were merely long, deep ditches, with steep snow walls on either side. Here and there you might hear the faint, far scrape of a wooden shovel, and if you were quick enough you might catch a glimpse of a distant black figure stooping and disappearing in one of those ditches, and reappearing the next moment with a motion which you would know meant the heaving out of a shovelful of snow. But you needed to be quick, for that black figure would not linger, but would soon drop that shovel and scud for the house, thrashing itself with its arms to warm them. Yes, it was too venomously cold for snow-shovelers or anybody else to stay out long.

Presently the sky darkened; then the wind rose and began to blow in fitful, vigorous gusts, which sent clouds of powdery snow aloft, and straight ahead, and everywhere. Under the impulse of one of these gusts, great white drifts banked themselves like graves across the streets; a moment later another gust shifted them around the other way, driving a fine spray of snow from their sharp crests, as the gale drives the spume flakes from wave-crests at sea; a third gust swept that place as clean as your hand, if it saw fit. This was fooling, this was play; but each and all of the gusts dumped some snow into the sidewalk ditches, for that was business.

Alonzo Fitz Clarence was sitting in his snug and elegant little parlor, in a lovely blue silk dressing-gown, with cuffs and facings of crimson satin, elaborately quilted. The remains of his breakfast were before him, and the dainty and costly little table service added a harmonious charm to the grace, beauty, and richness of the fixed appointments of the room. A cheery fire was blazing on the hearth.

A furious gust of wind shook the windows, and a great wave of snow washed against them with a drenching sound, so to speak. The handsome young bachelor murmured:

"That means, no going out to-day. Well, I am content. But what to do for company? Mother is well enough, Aunt Susan is well enough; but these, like the poor, I have with me always. On so grim a day as this, one needs a new interest, a fresh element, to whet the dull edge of captivity. That was very neatly said, but it doesn't mean anything.

One doesn't *want* the edge of captivity sharpened up, you know, but just the reverse."

He glanced at his pretty French mantel-clock.

"That clock's wrong again. That clock hardly ever knows what time it is; and when it does know, it lies about it—which amounts to the same thing. Alfred!"

There was no answer.

"Alfred! . . . Good servant, but as uncertain as the clock."

Alonzo touched an electric bell button in the wall. He waited a moment, then touched it again; waited a few moments more, and said:

"Battery out of order, no doubt. But now that I have started, I *will* find out what time it is." He stepped to a speaking-tube in the wall, blew its whistle, and called, "Mother!" and repeated it twice.

"Well, *that's* no use. Mother's battery is out of order, too. Can't raise anybody down-stairs—that is plain."

He sat down at a rosewood desk, leaned his chin on the left-hand edge of it and spoke, as if to the floor: "Aunt Susan!"

A low, pleasant voice answered, "Is that you, Alonzo?"

"Yes. I'm too lazy and comfortable to go down-stairs; I am in extremity, and I can't seem to scare up any help."

"Dear me, what is the matter?"

"Matter enough, I can tell you!"

"Oh, don't keep me in suspense, dear! What *is* it?"

"I want to know what time it is."

"You abominable boy, what a turn you did give me! Is that all?"

"All—on my honor. Calm yourself. Tell me the time, and receive my blessing."

"Just five minutes after nine. No charge—keep your blessing."

"Thanks. It wouldn't have impoverished me, aunty, nor so enriched you that you could live without other means."

He got up, murmuring, "Just five minutes after nine," and faced his clock. "Ah," said he, "you are doing better than usual. You are only thirty-four minutes wrong. Let me see . . . let me see. . . . Thirty-three and twenty-one are fifty-four; four times fifty-four are two hundred and thirty-six. One off, leaves two hundred and thirty-five. That's right."

He turned the hands of his clock forward till they marked twenty-five minutes to one, and said, "Now see if you can't keep right for a while . . . else I'll raffle you!"

He sat down at the desk again, and said, "Aunt Susan!"

"Yes, dear."

"Had breakfast?"

"Yes, indeed, an hour ago."

"Busy?"

"No—except sewing. Why?"

"Got any company?"

"No, but I expect some at half past nine."

"I wish *I* did. I'm lonesome. I want to talk to somebody."

"Very well, talk to me."

"But this is very private."

"Don't be afraid—talk right along, there's nobody here but me."

"I hardly know whether to venture or not, but—"

"But what? Oh, don't stop there! You *know* you can trust me, Alonzo—you know you can."

"I feel it, aunt, but this is very serious. It affects me deeply—me, and all the family—even the whole community."

"Oh, Alonzo, tell me! I will never breathe a word of it. What is it?"

"Aunt, if I might dare—"

"Oh, please go on! I love you, and feel for you. Tell me all. Confide in me. What *is* it?"

"The weather!"

"Plague take the weather! I don't see how you can have the heart to serve me so, Lon."

"There, there, aunty dear, I'm sorry; I am, on my honor. I won't do it again. Do you forgive me?"

"Yes, since you seem so sincere about it, though I know I oughtn't to. You will fool me again as soon as I have forgotten this time."

"No, I won't, honor bright. But such weather, oh, such weather! You've *got* to keep your spirits up artificially. It is snowy, and blowy, and gusty, and bitter cold! How is the weather with you?"

"Warm and rainy and melancholy. The mourners go about the streets with their umbrellas running streams from the end of every whalebone. There's an elevated double pavement of umbrellas stretching

down the sides of the streets as far as I can see.
I've got a fire for cheerfulness, and the windows open
to keep cool. But it is vain, it is useless: nothing
comes in but the balmy breath of December, with
its burden of mocking odors from the flowers that
possess the realm outside, and rejoice in their lawless
profusion whilst the spirit of man is low, and flaunt
their gaudy splendors in his face while his soul is
clothed in sackcloth and ashes and his heart
breaketh."

Alonzo opened his lips to say, "You ought to
print that, and get it framed," but checked himself,
for he heard his aunt speaking to some one else. He
went and stood at the window and looked out upon
the wintry prospect. The storm was driving the
snow before it more furiously than ever; window-
shutters were slamming and banging; a forlorn dog,
with bowed head and tail withdrawn from service,
was pressing his quaking body against a windward
wall for shelter and protection; a young girl was
plowing knee-deep through the drifts, with her face
turned from the blast, and the cape of her water-
proof blowing straight rearward over her head.
Alonzo shuddered, and said with a sigh, "Better the
slop, and the sultry rain, and even the insolent
flowers, than this!"

He turned from the window, moved a step, and
stopped in a listening attitude. The faint, sweet
notes of a familiar song caught his ear. He remained
there, with his head unconsciously bent forward,
drinking in the melody, stirring neither hand nor
foot, hardly breathing. There was a blemish in the

execution of the song, but to Alonzo it seemed an added charm instead of a defect. This blemish consisted of a marked flatting of the third, fourth, fifth, sixth, and seventh notes of the refrain or chorus of the piece. When the music ended, Alonzo drew a deep breath, and said, "Ah, I never have heard 'In the Sweet By-and-by' sung like that before!"

He stepped quickly to the desk, listened a moment, and said in a guarded, confidential voice, "Aunty, who is this divine singer?"

"She is the company I was expecting. Stays with me a month or two. I will introduce you. Miss—"

"For goodness' sake, wait a moment, Aunt Susan! You never stop to think what you are about!"

He flew to his bedchamber, and returned in a moment perceptibly changed in his outward appearance, and remarking, snappishly:

"Hang it, she would have introduced me to this angel in that sky-blue dressing-gown with red-hot lapels! Women never think, when they get a-going."

He hastened and stood by the desk, and said eagerly, "Now, Aunty, I am ready," and fell to smiling and bowing with all the persuasiveness and elegance that were in him.

"Very well. Miss Rosannah Ethelton, let me introduce to you my favorite nephew, Mr. Alonzo Fitz Clarence. There! You are both good people, and I like you; so I am going to trust you together while I attend to a few household affairs. Sit down, Rosannah; sit down, Alonzo. Good-by; I sha'n't be gone long."

Alonzo had been bowing and smiling all the while,

and motioning imaginary young ladies to sit down in
imaginary chairs, but now he took a seat himself,
mentally saying, "Oh, this is luck! Let the winds
blow now, and the snow drive, and the heavens
frown! Little I care!"

While these young people chat themselves into an
acquaintanceship, let us take the liberty of inspecting
the sweeter and fairer of the two. She sat alone, at
her graceful ease, in a richly furnished apartment
which was manifestly the private parlor of a refined
and sensible lady, if signs and symbols may go for
anything. For instance, by a low, comfortable chair
stood a dainty, top-heavy workstand, whose summit
was a fancifully embroidered shallow basket, with
varicolored crewels, and other strings and odds, and
ends protruding from under the gaping lid and
hanging down in negligent profusion. On the floor
lay bright shreds of Turkey red, Prussian blue, and
kindred fabrics, bits of ribbon, a spool or two, a
pair of scissors, and a roll or so of tinted silken stuffs.
On a luxurious sofa, upholstered with some sort of
soft Indian goods wrought in black and gold threads
interwebbed with other threads not so pronounced in
color, lay a great square of coarse white stuff, upon
whose surface a rich bouquet of flowers was growing,
under the deft cultivation of the crochet-needle. The
household cat was asleep on this work of art. In a
bay-window stood an easel with an unfinished picture
on it, and a palette and brushes on a chair beside it.
There were books everywhere: Robertson's Sermons,
Tennyson, Moody and Sankey, Hawthorne, *Rab
and his Friends*, cook-books, prayer-books, pattern-

books—and books about all kinds of odious and exasperating pottery, of course. There was a piano, with a deck-load of music, and more in a tender. There was a great plenty of pictures on the walls, on the shelves of the mantelpiece, and around generally; where coigns of vantage offered were statuettes, and quaint and pretty gimcracks, and rare and costly specimens of peculiarly devilish china. The bay-window gave upon a garden that was ablaze with foreign and domestic flowers and flowering shrubs.

But the sweet young girl was the daintiest thing these premises, within or without, could offer for contemplation: delicately chiseled features, of Grecian cast; her complexion the pure snow of a japonica that is receiving a faint reflected enrichment from some scarlet neighbor of the garden; great, soft blue eyes fringed with long, curving lashes; an expression made up of the trustfulness of a child and the gentleness of a fawn; a beautiful head crowned with its own prodigal gold; a lithe and rounded figure, whose every attitude and movement was instinct with native grace.

Her dress and adornment were marked by that exquisite harmony that can come only of a fine natural taste perfected by culture. Her gown was of a simple magenta tulle, cut bias, traversed by three rows of light-blue flounces, with the selvage edges turned up with ashes-of-roses chenille; overdress of dark bay tarlatan with scarlet satin lambrequins; corn-colored polonaise, *en panier*, looped with mother-of-pearl buttons and silver cord, and hauled aft and made fast by buff velvet lashings; basque of lavender reps, picked out with valenciennes; low neck, short sleeves; maroon velvet necktie edged with delicate pink silk; inside handkerchief of some simple three-ply ingrain fabric of a soft saffron tint; coral bracelets and locket-chain; coiffure of forget-me-nots and lilies-of-the-valley massed around a noble calla.

This was all; yet even in this subdued attire she was divinely beautiful. Then what must she have been when adorned for the festival or the ball?

All this time she had been busily chatting with Alonzo, unconscious of our inspection. The minutes still sped, and still she talked. But by and by she happened to look up, and saw the clock. A crimson blush sent its rich flood through her cheeks, and she exclaimed:

"There, good-by, Mr. Fitz Clarence; I must go now!"

She sprang from her chair with such haste that she hardly heard the young man's answering good-by. She stood radiant, graceful, beautiful, and gazed, wondering, upon the accusing clock. Presently her pouting lips parted, and she said:

"Five minutes after eleven! Nearly two hours, and it did not seem twenty minutes! Oh, dear, what will he think of me!"

At the self-same moment Alonzo was staring at *his* clock. And presently he said:

"Twenty-five minutes to three! Nearly two hours, and I didn't believe it was two minutes! Is it possible that this clock is humbugging again? Miss Ethelton! Just one moment, please. Are you there yet?"

"Yes, but be quick; I'm going right away."

"Would you be so kind as to tell me what time it is?"

The girl blushed again, murmured to herself, "It's right down cruel of him to ask me!" and then spoke up and answered with admirably counterfeited unconcern, "Five minutes after eleven."

"Oh, thank you! You have to go, now, have you?"

"Yes."

"I'm sorry."

No reply.

"Miss Ethelton!"

"Well?"

"You—you're there yet, *ain't* you?"

"Yes; but please hurry. What did you want to say?"

"Well, I—well, nothing in particular. It's very lonesome here. It's asking a great deal, I know, but would you mind talking with me again by and by— that is, if it will not trouble you too much?"

"I don't know—but I'll think about it. I'll try."

"Oh, thanks! Miss Ethelton! . . . Ah, me, she's gone, and here are the black clouds and the whirling snow and the raging winds come again! But she said *good-by*. She didn't say good morning, she said good-by! . . . The clock was right, after all. What a lightning-winged two hours it was!"

He sat down, and gazed dreamily into his fire for a while, then heaved a sigh and said:

"How wonderful it is! Two little hours ago I was a free man, and now my heart's in San Francisco!"

About that time Rosannah Ethelton, propped in the window-seat of her bedchamber, book in hand, was gazing vacantly out over the rainy seas that washed the Golden Gate, and whispering to herself, "How different he is from poor Burley, with his empty head and his single little antic talent of mimicry!"

II

FOUR weeks later Mr. Sidney Algernon Burley was entertaining a gay luncheon company, in a sumptuous drawing-room on Telegraph Hill, with some capital imitations of the voices and gestures of certain popular actors and San Franciscan literary people and Bonanza grandees. He was elegantly upholstered, and was a handsome fellow, barring a trifling cast in his eye. He seemed very jovial, but nevertheless he kept his eye on the door with an expectant and uneasy watchfulness. By and by a nobby lackey appeared, and delivered a message to the mistress, who nodded her head understandingly. That seemed to settle the thing for Mr. Burley; his vivacity decreased little by little, and a dejected look began to creep into one of his eyes and a sinister one into the other.

The rest of the company departed in due time, leaving him with the mistress, to whom he said:

"There is no longer any question about it. She avoids me. She continually excuses herself. If I could see her, if I could speak to her only a moment —but this suspense—"

"Perhaps her seeming avoidance is mere accident,

Mr. Burley. Go to the small drawing-room up-stairs and amuse yourself a moment. I will despatch a household order that is on my mind, and then I will go to her room. Without doubt she will be persuaded to see you."

Mr. Burley went up-stairs, intending to go to the small drawing-room, but as he was passing "Aunt Susan's" private parlor, the door of which stood slightly ajar, he heard a joyous laugh which he recognized; so without knock or announcement he stepped confidently in. But before he could make his presence known he heard words that harrowed up his soul and chilled his young blood. He heard a voice say:

"Darling, it has come!"

Then he heard Rosannah Ethelton, whose back was toward him, say:

"So has yours, dearest!"

He saw her bowed form bend lower; he heard her kiss something—not merely once, but again and again! His soul raged within him. The heart-breaking conversation went on:

"Rosannah, I knew you must be beautiful, but this is dazzling, this is blinding, this is intoxicating!"

"Alonzo, it is such happiness to hear you say it. I know it is not true, but I am *so* grateful to have you think it is, nevertheless! I knew you must have a noble face, but the grace and majesty of the reality beggar the poor creation of my fancy."

Burley heard that rattling shower of kisses again.

"Thank you, my Rosannah! The photograph

flatters me, but you must not allow yourself to think of that. Sweetheart?"

"Yes, Alonzo."

"I am so happy, Rosannah."

"Oh, Alonzo, none that have gone before me knew what love was, none that come after me will ever know what happiness is. I float in a gorgeous cloudland, a boundless firmament of enchanted and bewildering ecstasy!"

"Oh, my Rosannah!—for you are mine, are you not?"

"Wholly, oh, wholly yours, Alonzo, now and forever! All the day long, and all through my nightly dreams, one song sings itself, and its sweet burden is, 'Alonzo Fitz Clarence, Alonzo Fitz Clarence, Eastport, state of Maine!'"

"Curse him, I've got his address, anyway!" roared Burley, inwardly, and rushed from the place.

Just behind the unconscious Alonzo stood his mother, a picture of astonishment. She was so muffled from head to heel in furs that nothing of herself was visible but her eyes and nose. She was a good allegory of winter, for she was powdered all over with snow.

Behind the unconscious Rosannah stood "Aunt Susan," another picture of astonishment. She was a good allegory of summer, for she was lightly clad, and was vigorously cooling the perspiration on her face with a fan.

Both of these women had tears of joy in their eyes.

"So ho!" exclaimed Mrs. Fitz Clarence, "this explains why nobody has been able to drag you out of your room for six weeks, Alonzo!"

"So ho!" exclaimed Aunt Susan, "this explains why you have been a hermit for the past six weeks, Rosannah!"

The young couple were on their feet in an instant, abashed, and standing like detected dealers in stolen goods awaiting Judge Lynch's doom.

"Bless you, my son! I am happy in your happiness. Come to your mother's arms, Alonzo!"

"Bless you, Rosannah, for my dear nephew's sake! Come to my arms!"

Then was there a mingling of hearts and of tears of rejoicing on Telegraph Hill and in Eastport Square.

Servants were called by the elders, in both places. Unto one was given the order, "Pile this fire high with hickory wood, and bring me a roasting-hot lemonade."

Unto the other was given the order, "Put out this fire, and bring me two palm-leaf fans and a pitcher of ice-water."

Then the young people were dismissed, and the elders sat down to talk the sweet surprise over and make the wedding plans.

Some minutes before this Mr. Burley rushed from the mansion on Telegraph Hill without meeting or taking formal leave of anybody. He hissed through his teeth, in unconscious imitation of a popular favorite in melodrama, "Him shall she never wed! I have sworn it! Ere great Nature shall have doffed her winter's ermine to don the emerald gauds of spring, she shall be mine!"

III

Two weeks later. Every few hours, during some three or four days, a very prim and devout-looking Episcopal clergyman, with a cast in his eye, had visited Alonzo. According to his card, he was the Rev. Melton Hargrave, of Cincinnati. He said he had retired from the ministry on account of his health. If he had said on account of ill-health, he would probably have erred, to judge by his wholesome looks and firm build. He was the inventor of an improvement in telephones, and hoped to make his bread by selling the privilege of using it. "At present," he continued, "a man may go and tap a telegraph wire which is conveying a song or a concert from one state to another, and he can attach his private telephone and steal a hearing of that music as it passes along. My invention will stop all that."

"Well," answered Alonzo, "if the owner of the music could not miss what was stolen, why should he care?"

"He shouldn't care," said the Reverend.

"Well?" said Alonzo, inquiringly.

"Suppose," replied the Reverend, "suppose that, instead of music that was passing along and being stolen, the burden of the wire was loving endearments of the most private and sacred nature?"

Alonzo shuddered from head to heel. "Sir, it is a priceless invention," said he; "I must have it at any cost."

But the invention was delayed somewhere on the

road from Cincinnati, most unaccountably. The impatient Alonzo could hardly wait. The thought of Rosannah's sweet words being shared with him by some ribald thief was galling to him. The Reverend came frequently and lamented the delay, and told of measures he had taken to hurry things up. This was some little comfort to Alonzo.

One forenoon the Reverend ascended the stairs and knocked at Alonzo's door. There was no response. He entered, glanced eagerly around, closed the door softly, then ran to the telephone. The exquisitely soft and remote strains of the "Sweet By-and-by" came floating through the instrument. The singer was flatting, as usual, the five notes that follow the first two in the chorus, when the Reverend interrupted her with this word, in a voice which was an exact imitation of Alonzo's, with just the faintest flavor of impatience added:

"Sweetheart?"

"Yes, Alonzo?"

"Please don't sing that any more this week—try something modern."

The agile step that goes with a happy heart was heard on the stairs, and the Reverend, smiling diabolically, sought sudden refuge behind the heavy folds of the velvet window-curtains. Alonzo entered and flew to the telephone. Said he:

"Rosannah, dear, shall we sing something together?"

"Something *modern?*" asked she, with sarcastic bitterness.

"Yes, if you prefer."

"Sing it yourself, if you like!"

This snappishness amazed and wounded the young man. He said:

"Rosannah, that was not like you."

"I suppose it becomes me as much as your very polite speech became you, Mr. Fitz Clarence."

"*Mister* Fitz Clarence! Rosannah, there was nothing impolite about my speech."

"Oh, indeed! Of course, then, I misunderstood you, and I most humbly beg your pardon, ha-ha-ha! No doubt you said, 'Don't sing it any more *to-day.*'"

"Sing *what* any more to-day?"

"The song you mentioned, of course. How very obtuse we are, all of a sudden!"

"I never mentioned any song."

"Oh, you *didn't?*"

"No, I *didn't!*"

"I am compelled to remark that you *did.*"

"And I am obliged to reiterate that I *didn't.*"

"A second rudeness! That is sufficient, sir. I will never forgive you. All is over between us."

Then came a muffled sound of crying. Alonzo hastened to say:

"Oh, Rosannah, unsay those words! There is some dreadful mystery here, some hideous mistake. I am utterly earnest and sincere when I say I never said anything about any song. I would not hurt you for the whole world. . . . Rosannah, dear! . . . Oh, speak to me, won't you?"

There was a pause; then Alonzo heard the girl's sobbings retreating, and knew she had gone from the telephone. He rose with a heavy sigh, and hastened from the room, saying to himself, "I will ransack the charity missions and the haunts of the poor for my mother. She will persuade her that I never meant to wound her."

A minute later the Reverend was crouching over the telephone like a cat that knoweth the ways of the prey. He had not very many minutes to wait. A soft, repentant voice, tremulous with tears, said:

"Alonzo, dear, I have been wrong. You *could* not have said so cruel a thing. It must have been some one who imitated your voice in malice or in jest."

The Reverend coldly answered, in Alonzo's tones:

"You have said all was over between us. So let it be. I spurn your proffered repentance, and despise it!"

Then he departed, radiant with fiendish triumph, to return no more with his imaginary telephonic invention forever.

Four hours afterward Alonzo arrived with his mother from her favorite haunts of poverty and vice. They summoned the San Francisco household; but there was no reply. They waited, and continued to wait, upon the voiceless telephone.

At length, when it was sunset in San Francisco, and three hours and a half after dark in Eastport, an answer to the oft-repeated cry of "Rosannah!"

But, alas, it was Aunt Susan's voice that spake. She said:

"I have been out all day; just got in. I will go and find her."

The watchers waited two minutes—five minutes—ten minutes. Then came these fatal words, in a frightened tone:

"She is gone, and her baggage with her. To visit another friend, she told the servants. But I found this note on the table in her room. Listen: 'I am gone; seek not to trace me out; my heart is broken; you will never see me more. Tell him I shall always think of him when I sing my poor "Sweet By-and-by," but never of the unkind words he said about it.' That is her note. Alonzo, Alonzo, what does it mean? What has happened?"

But Alonzo sat white and cold as the dead. His mother threw back the velvet curtains and opened a window. The cold air refreshed the sufferer, and he told his aunt his dismal story. Meantime his mother was inspecting a card which had disclosed itself upon the floor when she cast the curtains back. It read, "Mr. Sidney Algernon Burley, San Francisco."

"The miscreant!" shouted Alonzo, and rushed forth to seek the false Reverend and destroy him; for the card explained everything, since in the course of the lovers' mutual confessions they had told each other all about all the sweethearts they had ever had, and thrown no end of mud at their failings and foibles—for lovers always do that. It has a fascination that ranks next after billing and cooing.

IV

During the next two months many things happened. It had early transpired that Rosannah, poor suffering orphan, had neither returned to her grandmother in Portland, Oregon, nor sent any word to her save a duplicate of the woeful note she had left in the mansion on Telegraph Hill. Whosoever was sheltering her—if she was still alive—had been persuaded not to betray her whereabouts, without doubt; for all efforts to find trace of her had failed.

Did Alonzo give her up? Not he. He said to himself, "She will sing that sweet song when she is sad; I shall find her." So he took his carpet-sack and a portable telephone, and shook the snow of his native city from his arctics, and went forth into the world. He wandered far and wide and in many states. Time and again, strangers were astounded to see a wasted, pale, and woe-worn man laboriously climb a telegraph-pole in wintry and lonely places, perch sadly there an hour, with his ear at a little box, then come sighing down, and wander wearily away. Sometimes they shot at him, as peasants do at aeronauts, thinking him mad and dangerous. Thus his clothes were much shredded by bullets and his person grievously lacerated. But he bore it all patiently.

In the beginning of his pilgrimage he used often to say, "Ah, if I could but hear the 'Sweet By-and-by'!" But toward the end of it he used to shed tears of anguish and say, "Ah, if I could but hear something else!"

Thus a month and three weeks drifted by, and at last some humane people seized him and confined him in a private mad-house in New York. He made no moan, for his strength was all gone, and with it all heart and all hope. The superintendent, in pity, gave up his own comfortable parlor and bedchamber to him and nursed him with affectionate devotion.

At the end of a week the patient was able to leave his bed for the first time. He was lying, comfortably pillowed, on a sofa, listening to the plaintive Miserere of the bleak March winds and the muffled sound of tramping feet in the street below—for it was about six in the evening, and New York was going home from work. He had a bright fire and the added cheer of a couple of student-lamps. So it was warm and snug within, though bleak and raw without; it was light and bright within, though outside it was as dark and dreary as if the world had been lit with Hartford gas. Alonzo smiled feebly to think how his loving vagaries had made him a maniac in the eyes of the world, and was proceeding to pursue his line of thought further, when a faint, sweet strain, the very ghost of sound, so remote and attenuated it seemed, struck upon his ear. His pulses stood still; he listened with parted lips and bated breath. The song flowed on—he waiting, listening, rising slowly and unconsciously from his recumbent position. At last he exclaimed:

"It is! it is she! Oh, the divine flatted notes!"

He dragged himself eagerly to the corner whence the sounds proceeded, tore aside a curtain, and discovered a telephone. He bent over, and as the last note died away he burst forth with the exclamation:

"Oh, thank Heaven, found at last! Speak to me, Rosannah, dearest! The cruel mystery has been unraveled; it was the villain Burley who mimicked my voice and wounded you with insolent speech!"

There was a breathless pause, a waiting age to

Alonzo; then a faint sound came, framing itself into language:

"Oh, say those precious words again, Alonzo!"

"They are the truth, the veritable truth, my Rosannah, and you shall have the proof, ample and abundant proof!"

"Oh, Alonzo, stay by me! Leave me not for a moment! Let me feel that you are near me! Tell me we shall never be parted more! Oh, this happy hour, this blessed hour, this memorable hour!"

"We will make record of it, my Rosannah; every year, as this dear hour chimes from the clock, we will celebrate it with thanksgivings, all the years of our life."

"We will, we will, Alonzo!"

"Four minutes after six, in the evening, my Rosannah, shall henceforth—"

"Twenty-three minutes after twelve, afternoon, shall—"

"Why, Rosannah, darling, where are you?"

"In Honolulu, Sandwich Islands. And where are you? Stay by me; do not leave me for a moment. I cannot bear it. Are you at home?"

"No, dear, I am in New York—a patient in the doctor's hands."

An agonizing shriek came buzzing to Alonzo's ear, like the sharp buzzing of a hurt gnat; it lost power in traveling five thousand miles. Alonzo hastened to say:

"Calm yourself, my child. It is nothing. Already I am getting well under the sweet healing of your presence. Rosannah?"

"Yes, Alonzo? Oh, how you terrified me! Say on."

"Name the happy day, Rosannah!"

There was a little pause. Then a diffident small voice replied, "I blush—but it is with pleasure, it is with happiness. Would—would you like to have it soon?"

"This very night, Rosannah! Oh, let us risk no more delays. Let it be now!—this very night, this very moment!"

"Oh, you impatient creature! I have nobody here but my good old uncle, a missionary for a generation, and now retired from service—nobody but him and his wife. I would so dearly like it if your mother and your Aunt Susan—"

"*Our* mother and *our* Aunt Susan, my Rosannah."

"Yes, *our* mother and *our* Aunt Susan—I am content to word it so if it pleases you; I would so like to have them present."

"So would I. Suppose you telegraph Aunt Susan. How long would it take her to come?"

"The steamer leaves San Francisco day after to-morrow. The passage is eight days. She would be here the 31st of March."

"Then name the 1st of April; do, Rosannah, dear."

"Mercy, it would make us April fools, Alonzo!"

"So we be the happiest ones that that day's sun looks down upon in the whole broad expanse of the globe, why need we care? Call it the 1st of April, dear."

'Then the 1st of April it shall be, with all my heart!"

"Oh, happiness! Name the hour, too, Rosannah."

"I like the morning, it is so blithe. Will eight in the morning do, Alonzo?"

"The loveliest hour in the day—since it will make you mine."

There was a feeble but frantic sound for some little time, as if wool-lipped, disembodied spirits were exchanging kisses; then Rosannah said, "Excuse me just a moment, dear; I have an appointment, and am called to meet it."

The young girl sought a large parlor and took her place at a window which looked out upon a beautiful scene. To the left one could view the charming Nuuana Valley, fringed with its ruddy flush of tropical flowers and its plumed and graceful cocoa palms; its rising foothills clothed in the shining green of lemon, citron, and orange groves; its storied precipice beyond, where the first Kamehameha drove his defeated foes over to their destruction—a spot that had forgotten its grim history, no doubt, for now it was smiling, as almost always at noonday, under the glowing arches of a succession of rainbows. In front of the window one could see the quaint town, and here and there a picturesque group of dusky natives, enjoying the blistering weather; and far to the right lay the restless ocean, tossing its white mane in the sunshine.

Rosannah stood there, in her filmy white raiment, fanning her flushed and heated face, waiting. A Kanaka boy, clothed in a damaged blue necktie and part of a silk hat, thrust his head in at the door, and announced, "'Frisco *haole!*"

"Show him in," said the girl, straightening herself up and assuming a meaning dignity. Mr. Sidney Algernon Burley entered, clad from head to heel in dazzling snow—that is to say, in the lightest and whitest of Irish linen. He moved eagerly forward, but the girl made a gesture and gave him a look which checked him suddenly. She said, coldly, "I am here, as I promised. I believed your assertions, I yielded to your importunities, and said I would name the day. I name the 1st of April—eight in the morning. Now go!"

"Oh, my dearest, if the gratitude of a lifetime—"

"Not a word. Spare me all sight of you, all communication with you, until that hour. No—no supplications; I will have it so."

When he was gone, she sank exhausted in a chair, for the long siege of troubles she had undergone had wasted her strength. Presently she said, "What a narrow escape! If the hour appointed had been an hour earlier—Oh, horror, what an escape I have made! And to think I had come to imagine I was loving this beguiling, this truthless, this treacherous monster! Oh, he shall repent his villainy!"

Let us now draw this history to a close, for little more needs to be told. On the 2d of the ensuing April, the Honolulu *Advertiser* contained this notice:

MARRIED.—In this city, by telephone, yesterday morning, at eight o'clock, by Rev. Nathan Hays, assisted by Rev. Nathaniel Davis, of New York, Mr. Alonzo Fitz Clarence, of Eastport, Maine, U. S., and Miss Rosannah Ethelton, of Portland, Oregon, U. S. Mrs. Susan Howland, of San Francisco, a friend of the bride, was present, she being the guest of the Rev. Mr. Hays and wife, uncle and aunt of the bride. Mr. Sidney Algernon Burley, of San Francisco, was also present but did not remain till the conclusion of the marriage service. Captain Hawthorne's beautiful yacht, tastefully decorated, was in waiting, and the happy bride and her friends immediately departed on a bridal trip to Lahaina and Haleakala.

The New York papers of the same date contained this notice:

MARRIED.—In this city, yesterday, by telephone, at half-past two in the morning, by Rev. Nathaniel Davis, assisted by Rev. Nathan Hays, of Honolulu, Mr. Alonzo Fitz Clarence, of Eastport, Maine, and Miss Rosannah Ethelton, of Portland, Oregon. The parents and several friends of the bridegroom were present, and enjoyed a sumptuous breakfast and much festivity until nearly sunrise, and then departed on a bridal trip to the Aquarium, the bridegroom's state of health not admitting of a more extended journey.

Toward the close of that memorable day Mr. and Mrs. Alonzo Fitz Clarence were buried in sweet converse concerning the pleasures of their several bridal tours, when suddenly the young wife exclaimed: "Oh, Lonny, I forgot! I did what I said I would."

"Did you, dear?"

"Indeed, I did. I made *him* the April fool! And I told him so, too! Ah, it was a charming surprise! There he stood, sweltering in a black dress-suit, with the mercury leaking out of the top of the thermometer, waiting to be married. You should have seen the look he gave when I whispered it in his ear. Ah, his wickedness cost me many a heartache and many a tear, but the score was all squared up, then. So the vengeful feeling went right out of my heart, and I begged him to stay, and said I forgave him everything. But he wouldn't. He said he would live to be avenged; said he would make our lives a curse to us. But he can't, *can* he, dear?"

"Never in this world, my Rosannah!"

Aunt Susan, the Oregonian grandmother, and the young couple and their Eastport parents, are all happy at this writing, and likely to remain so. Aunt Susan brought the bride from the islands, accompanied her across our continent, and had the happiness of witnessing the rapturous meeting between an adoring husband and wife who had never seen each other until that moment.

A word about the wretched Burley, whose wicked machinations came so near wrecking the hearts and lives of our poor young friends, will be sufficient. In a murderous attempt to seize a crippled and helpless artisan who he fancied had done him some small offense, he fell into a caldron of boiling oil and expired before he could be extinguished.

This Book
belongs to

_____

_____